BORIS KARLOFF PRESENTS

more

TALES OF THE FRIGHTENED

Text by

Robert Lory

PYRAMID BOOKS NEW YORK

BORIS KARLOFF PRESENTS
MORE TALES OF THE FRIGHTENED

Produced by Lyle Kenyon Engel

A PYRAMID BOOK

Pyramid edition published February 1975
Second printing, March 1975

ISBN 0-515-03716-8

Library of Congress Catalog Card Number: 74-29421

Printed in the United States of America

Pyramid Books are published by Pyramid Communications, Inc. Its trademarks, consisting of the word "Pyramid" and the portrayal of a pyramid, are registered in the United States Patent Office.

Pyramid Communications, Inc.,
919 Third Avenue,
New York, N.Y. 10022

CONTENTS

BORIS KARLOFF

PRESENTS more

TALES OF THE FRIGHTENED

HEARTTHROB

The story of Duane Winsome

I so detest pushy people, don't you? I mean the kind of people who just won't let you be alone, but who insist on forcing themselves upon you. Duane Winsome was such a person, but he learned his lesson. In any event, I think he did . . . he certainly *should* have. . . .

In the Los Angeles office building where Duane Winsome worked, he knew almost all of the young ladies by name, the pretty ones at least. He had dated most of them, not that they had willingly gone out with him. It was just that, well, he was that type of man. He simply wouldn't take no for an answer. He was a good-looking young man and intelligent too, but he did have one serious blind spot in his makeup. He simply could not comprehend that there was any woman on this earth, let alone Los Angeles, who would not want to spend an evening with one Duane Winsome.

9

So it was with his usual arrogance that he carried his tray to a particular table in the building's ground-floor cafeteria and sat down uninvited across from the raven-haired young woman who seemed to be toying with her cup of black coffee. He was, of course, quick to introduce himself and just as quick to observe aloud that he'd not seen her here before. She on her part merely said that she didn't work in the building. She just thought she'd try out the food here. Her eyes, however, communicated the fact that she wished Duane Winsome would take his tray and himself to some other table. Or they would have communicated that fact—to anyone other than Duane Winsome. On his part, he was eager for a date with this lovely—which she really was. It was only when she refused to accompany him that evening to, in order of mention, a movie, a stage show, a friend's party, a walk about town, and an evening at home—his—that he thought to ask the young lady why. Did she already have an engagement? Perhaps tomorrow night would be better?

No, she told him. She had no engagement tonight, but—no—tomorrow night would be no better. It was her mother. Her voice tinkled like notes from a dainty silver bell as she told him: "I can go out with no one until Mother gives her approval, and for the time being she has had her fill of my men friends."

"But she has not met *me!*" Duane insisted, satisfying himself that it would be not much of a chore to set the girl's mother at ease. No doubt the old woman's interest was right in terms of some of the riffraff who probably pushed themselves at her lovely daughter's feet. But he, after all, was Duane Winsome. The mother, as well as the daughter, would recognize his intrinsic qualities. Yet the girl seemed unsure. Nonetheless, he advanced his argument forcefully—with the fullness of his force, that is—and finally the girl

10

could do little except stare openmouthed at his power. He knew the moment when it came, knew that he'd be accompanying her home this evening. And after that . . . well, he would see about that.

Indeed he would.

When the taxi dropped them in front of the old wooden building in an ancient neighborhood which Duane never had ventured into before, he was surprised. "Privacy," the girl said softly. "Mother and I like privacy." Well, he thought to himself, this certainly was the place to get it. The buildings, all of them including the one which they were now approaching, should have been condemned a long time ago. As she unlocked and opened the door, he noted that there seemed to be very little light in the interior. And the dust—

"Ararg!" he said, startled as he stepped into the foyer and into the mass of cobwebs. The girl looked back at him, but said nothing. He shrugged, resigned to the filthy state of the housekeeping, and stepped after her. He did so for exactly six paces. Then he found he couldn't move. His legs and arms were so entwined by the gray-spun cobwebs that he could move neither forward nor backward. It was then the girl again turned and came toward him. Behind her was something Duane at first thought was her shadow. It wasn't. It evidenced movement of its own. Low to the ground it was, a thing which looked like the giant form of some shell one might find at the beach. Well, it would have looked that way were it not for the six, long, thin, red-colored legs which moved it forward. "Mother," the girl said by way of introduction.

Well, you can imagine just how vigorously Duane Winsome fought against the strands which held him. Alas, it was all to no avail. After he relaxed in a state of exhaustion, he looked up to see the girl's eyes shin-

11

ing bright before him.

"As I said, Mother has had her fill of my men friends for the time being. Fortunately, you will keep. . . ."

It is in the remembered echoes of Duane Winsome's shrieking that I consider your invitation to dinner this evening—the invitation I have tried politely to decline but which now you have left me little alternative but to accept. I do accept it, but on one condition. That I am allowed to bring . . . someone . . . with me. . . .

BLOOD WILL TELL

The story of Albert Winston

You know, of course, that the majority of murders
are crimes. Not of premeditation but of passion. But
did you ever stop to think why? Think about it now.
Think of yourself committing the conscious act of
snuffing out the life of another human being—planning every step. Making sure that the execution was
such that you would not be found out. And then performing with your own hands the execution itself. A
decidedly grisly affair. One which not very many of
us would be capable of. So it was with Albert
Winston, who could not bring himself to murder his
wife, but then went on to do so anyway . . . with mad-
dening results. . . .

Albert and Cora Winston had been married for
twenty-three years. It was a childless marriage, but
not because they had planned it that way. They had
in fact neither planned to have children nor planned

not to have them. It was, to Albert Winston, symbolic of their entire span of years together. Nothing had been planned. Not the tedious clerical job at which he worked in spite of Cora's substantial inheritance. Not the huge dark house they lived in and which a goodly part of that inheritance had financed. Not even the gardens in which Cora worked daily but in such a disorganized way that, while the various flower plots looked satisfactory in themselves, the overall effect appeared visually disturbing. It was, in a way, quite . . . insane.

That, at least, was how Albert Winston thought of the garden. Insane. And that is how he came to think of all aspects of his life with Cora. Oh, he didn't romanticize about having a woman who was more beautiful than the plain, bland Cora. No, he didn't do that at all. He recognized that he himself was as plain and bland as she was, perhaps even more so. Nonetheless, more and more, he felt the need to be free of her. She and everything about her, all of it was driving him insane. Yet, he knew he could not just pick up and leave her. Albert Winston was not imaginative enough even to dream of where he might go, what he might do. No, he would not leave his home, his town, his job. Therefore, there was only one solution and that was that Cora must die. Very simple, then. Albert would murder her.

He planned very carefully, very methodically. But like Albert, very unimaginatively. He would dig a hole in the garden, lure Cora out there, kill her with a meat cleaver. Then use the meat cleaver to chop up her body into little pieces which would be buried in the garden. All of it was so simple. Albert Winston was certain it would work and that he would not be caught. There was only one problem. When the night came, when the very hour of the night came that he was to put his careful plan into action, he couldn't do

14

it. He was outside in the garden, the spade dug into its first clump of soft dark soil, when he knew he couldn't go through with it. At that moment, perhaps, Albert's mind snapped. He could not murder, but he had to get away from his wife. He could not, would not move to another place. So to his mind there came but one solution. He would commit suicide.

Again, Albert was most unimaginative. Right before the kitchen drawer from which he took the meat cleaver which had been meant for Cora, he sliced his left wrist. Because he blacked out before completing the job, he was not very thorough, and when Cora found him he still was alive. Plenty of time to get him to the hospital and to replace in his system the quantity of blood he had lost. He was back home in almost no time at all, no one even thinking that the mishap was anything other than an accident.

He had failed at murder and he had failed at suicide. So Albert Winston resigned himself to his unbearable status quo. Which would have been the end of our story had not Cora confided to him one night something about the blood which had saved his life. It was about nine and they were in the garden. She had been using the spade, digging a hole much like the one Albert had planned to use for her grave when his thoughts were those of the murderous husband. Some kind of bush she was planting, one which required deep roots. And then she said the thing which sent Albert stalking silently back into the house.

"The blood," she said. "The blood you received at the hospital. It was mine, you know. I wanted to do what I could to save you, and the doctor said I was of the same type."

She had expected, perhaps, a word of thanks from Albert, but instead he was in a state of shock. And when he came out of the house . . .

15

He had the cleaver with him. She screamed bloody murder, Cora Winston did, but Albert finished her off with slices the power of which amazed even him. When the deed was done, it took him no time at all to cover her with earth. He even set in the two pieces of shrubbery that Cora had planned for the spot.

Neighbors being what they are, the screams were reported to the authorities. Within the hour two policemen stood at Albert's door. He greeted them with a smile. The smile was not only the external expression on his face—no, he really *felt* good all over, deep inside. Of course, they wanted to check the house and the grounds as well. Naturally, Albert said they could do as they wished, also saying he had no idea where his wife was. She had said flatly she was leaving him. He was cordial and kind, the model of a good and cooperative citizen—even when they reached that place in the garden, the place where Cora lay buried. And then . . .

The taller of the two policemen stared in wonder at the earth. "Blood," he said. "Fresh blood!" It was impossible! So thought Albert, but then he looked at the soil. There *was* fresh blood there. Yet he'd turned the earth so carefully. Then as the tall policeman called to the other to get a shovel, Albert saw it. He saw where the blood was coming from. His left wrist . . . it was dripping . . . dripping the blood which Cora had given him . . . dripping down to the place where Cora lay.

An odd story? Albert Winston doesn't think so. Not that he places much value in what the police said in their report after they found Cora's body. They conjectured he'd cut himself accidentally on something on the way out to the garden. Just luck, Albert's bad luck, that the blood happened to drip where it did. And Albert's explanation? Perhaps he has one, but he's not telling. He's not telling anyone anything.

16

He just sits there in his white-walled room, staring at nothing at all. There is, on his face, what might be a half smile. If that is what it is, perhaps it's there because, finally, Albert has escaped.

THE FORBIDDEN PAGE

The story of Charles Dell

I so admire artists, don't you? The ability to look at a blank canvas and see something there which at that particular moment is but a mental image, and then, with deft strokes of brush and paint, to transfer the mental to the visual. . . . Please, look up from that book you're holding for a moment to hear of another book. A book containing paintings, one of the pages of which—

But I get ahead of myself. I should begin by telling you that Charles Dell was a bit of an artist himself. Not a very accomplished one, I must admit. But like many painters at his level of talent he liberally stole ideas from past artists. Thus by repainting their ideas he managed to keep himself just a bit beyond the state of poverty. For the people who buy paintings—even in sophisticated New York City where Charles painted and sold—are not always as knowledgeable about such things as they might be. Part of the reason, of course, was that Charles did not copy the works of well-known painters. No, he was much too smart for that. But the works of the obscure are not all that available for study, and thus Charles became a familiar haunt of the old and dusty used bookstores which are found on Manhattan's lower half.

It was a rainy day in September when Charles Dell noticed a store he'd never seen before, at least to his knowledge. It was, then, with a spirit of anticipation that he approached the narrow building and tried the door. For a moment he was under the impression that it was locked, but he was wrong. The door swung open easily, closing softly behind him as he entered. The long single room was hardly illuminated, the table upon table of books looking quite strange in their rows. It seemed as if there was no one in the place to assist him, but then that impression too was seen to be incorrect as, suddenly from somewhere behind Charles, a man with a gaunt face and wispy beard appeared. The man was smiling as if he recognized Charles, and indeed he did.

"Ah, Mr. Dell," he said, his voice almost a whisper. "It is good of you to come." When Charles expressed surprise that his name should be known by the other man, the proprietor inclined his head. "You are an artist," he said. "I have seen much of your work. Much in the style of Claude Durham, I think."

Charles Dell's heart almost stopped. Claude Durham—yes, his Claude Durham was a nineteenth-century watercolorist who had specialized in works which bordered upon the grotesque. Charles's style for many paintings was much like that artist's. He had stolen liberally from every piece of Durham's work that he could find. Unfortunately, it had been more than two years since Charles had seen anything new at all by the long-dead artist.

And then he heard the words which thrilled him. The bookseller was saying that he had a special bound folio of Durham's work—a very limited edition, the man said. Would Mr. Dell like to see it? There was no question about it. It was in his hands but for a moment when Charles knew from the first two paintings in the folio that he'd seen none of this work before. His hands gripped the binding as if they were vises. He would own this folio, regardless of the price.

As it happened, the price was far below what Charles had expected it to be. Curious, though, was the comment of the bookseller as he gave Charles his change. "For you, Mr. Dell," he said, "I have made a special price. I know that Claude Durham himself would want you to have this work." And then, a strange look coming over the man's face, he said something with a tone of warning, "Number 14, Mr. Dell. Do not under any circumstances look at that page."

Charles, convinced that the man was mad, nonetheless assured him that he would do as warned. As he left the store, he saw that it still was raining, and, in order not to get his new possession wet, he hailed a taxi. Normally taxis were considered to be too expensive a mode of transportation for Charles, but today . . . well, the thing he had under his arm would put him in the money for some time to come. As he entered the rear of the cab, he was overjoyed to find that there were some forty pieces in the folio. Forty . . . counting that one he was warned against. Number 14, the bearded man had said. Number 14, Charles Dell thought to himself . . . that one must truly be a masterpiece. No sooner had he given the particulars of his address to the taxi driver than he opened the book and leafed through the first pages.

Yes . . . yes . . . the same grosteque hand of Durham. The weird grays and greens, the wild blacks and blues, the bloodlike reds. Page after page flipped over, and suddenly Charles realized he was looking down at Number 13, a curious picture of a fanged gargoyle chewing on what looked to be a human skull. His fingers trembled as they prepared to turn to the next page . . . they trembled and stopped, as if of their own will they did not wish to perform the action. "Foolish!" Charles muttered to himself—and he turned the page.

Odd. . . . There seemed to be nothing on it. It seemed to be totally blank. No, that wasn't quite true. It was as if the painting were executed in a very watered-down brown ink, but it could be made out—barely—as he brought the page closer to his eyes. There was a face . . . a laughing face. The face of . . . of the thin, bearded man in the bookstore! And below that face there was a single word, in darkening black Gothic letters. THIEF! Charles Dell screamed. He screamed once, twice, he screamed ever so much. But the taxi driver only heard the first cry, none of the others.

The authorities were as puzzled as the driver who claimed that, one moment there was a man screaming in the rear of his cab, and the next there was no one. Nothing except the book of artwork the man had been carrying. If it hadn't been for that, there would have been nothing at all to substantiate the driver's wild tale. Of course, if the driver had bothered to leaf through the book . . . if he would have paused to give due attention to Number 14, he might have been ever more puzzled. He no doubt would have recognized the face of the man on that page . . . . the man who seemed to be screaming for all he was worth. . . .

Yes, artists can be vindictive people, it's true. But I have found the same thing to be true of certain writers. That book you're holding now, for example . . . are you sure that you want to turn that next page?

GRAINS OF DEATH

The story of Frankie Ventura

We've all heard about occupational stress. That's when the doctor peers at his little charts after your physical examination, peers and shakes his head a little, and advises you that you need a vacation. Get away from it all, all those pressures, go to some beach resort perhaps, lie in the sun and relax. If you don't, if you keep on the way you're going . . . well, doctors do have a way of sounding like funeral directors sometimes, don't they? And yet the cure they recommend sometimes is far worse than the ailment. Such was the case with Frankie Ventura, but of course Frankie's occupational stress was perhaps greater than yours or mine, due to the nature of his occupation.

Nonetheless, that afternoon as he lay on an almost deserted stretch of Florida sand, Frankie Ventura vowed that he'd make every attempt to get body and mind back into a state of equilibrium. The last job had been particularly unnerving. Every time he closed his eyes at night—or now behind his dark sunglasses—he could see the face of the man, the horrified man whose eyes widened in terror at the sight of Frankie's big automatic, the man whose well-tanned face turned a pale, jaundiced yellow at the sight of his own death coming at him . . . and then that same face losing all shape as the slugs from Frankie's gun smashed into its center just to the right of the man's nose, splattering bone and brain matter in blood-drenched explosions every which way. A very sloppy killing, it had been, but that's the way it had been ordered up. The man who had assigned Frankie the contract wanted the kill to demonstrate the seriousness of crossing the organization.

But that haunting face . . . And lately too there were other faces, not as torn apart as that last one, but faces which were in their own way distorted in death. Gray faces . . . moaning like some lonely wind . . . faces which seemed to loom over misshapen bodies, the hands of which seemed to be grasping outward, forward, gnarled gray fingers reaching toward . . .

He woke up with a start, the sweat caused by the heat of the afternoon sun stinging his eyes, his right hand moving up to adjust his sunglasses. His head snapped up in fright as he realized that something was holding down his right hand, dragging on it, grasping it with a clutch of death!

And then he laughed at himself and at the two
26

small boys, the older of the two no more than four or five, the two boys with their sand buckets and shovels who systematically had been covering his body with the fine grains of sand. At first they looked frightened of him, but when he didn't yell at them they laughed back at him. "Where's your mother?" he asked them, turning about and looking up and down the beach. One of the boys pointed. In three or four places farther up the beach sat individual women, reading, knitting, or just looking at the sea. "She told us not to bother you," the second boy said. "She said that you probably would get mad at us." One of the women Frankie had been looking at now stood, her body an excellent one. She waved to him. He waved back, then told the kids to continue their work. The cooling sensation of the sand felt good in any case and, it just might be that after the boys had dinner and were in bed, Frankie and the mother might hit it off together. Florida, after all, was full of young divorcees. . . .

He closed his eyes, trying to think what the woman might look like close up, feeling the small shovels of sand drop their tiny loads upon his arms and his trunk and his legs. So cool, so very cool. . . . And then his dreams were disturbed once more by those faces of dead men, those pale faces which now seemed to be coming closer, their twisted fingers reaching out toward him, fingers as cold as ice. . . .

He woke then, a shiver of dread running down his spine. His eyes at first could not comprehend the grayness, and then he realized that he must have been asleep for some time. The sun was low in the sky and its rays were almost completely blocked by shroudlike clouds. A bolt of fear shot through him, but it wasn't until he tried to rise that he found himself to be in real panic. He could not rise . . . he could not move any part of his body. Only his head could he turn, the rest of him was covered by a huge and

27

crushingly heavy mound of sand. Those kids . . .

But they were nowhere to be seen. In fact there was no one on the beach at all—no one except the woman who spoke from behind him, the woman he could not see because his head would not turn in that one backward direction.

"I told the boys I would finish, Mr. Ventura," she said. Her voice was as cold as the sand which now was unbearable upon his body. He tried to struggle upward, but he knew it was useless. And then he understood. This woman and her children, they had belonged to one of those he had killed. But which one—*which* one? Even now as, in the back of his mind those gray moaning faces and those fingers of death came ever closer, he had to know. "*Which one?*" he cried.

But he gagged upon the last word, the small particles of sand which fell from the suddenly appearing bucket, its bright red and yellow colors looking dull and deadly in the smothered gray light, those particles of sand entering his mouth, flowing down to the base of his tongue, choking as they reached his windpipe. As well-tanned fingers removed his sunglasses, he again tried to scream, and this time the grains of sand dropped grittily into his eyes as well as his mouth. And he knew now that she would not speak to him again, that she would not tell him for whom her act of vengeance was performed. But as the grains of sand followed grains of sand, into his eyes, his nose, his mouth, one of the gray faces which haunted him in his dreams came closer than the others. He strained to recognize it, but before he could his brain was bathed in a blood-drenching explosion of choking and heaving, as within his chest his lungs burst and collapsed in agonizing death.

Do you feel overworked? Are the pressures of your job getting to be just a little too much? Consider the

28

beach, my friend. It can be most relaxful, even on the darkest of days. But do be careful of little boys, especially if they approach you, their little hands grasping tightly little buckets and sand shovels. . . .

THE TERROR BLEND

The story of Malcolm Hatch

I know, you would love to give up smoking, you really wish you could free yourself of the habit . . . if only you had the required amount of willpower, you say. Fortunately, if you are serious in your wish, there are a number of methods and products which can be of effective assistance. Do be careful, though, in your selection. And be sure to follow that age-old advice which appears on a variety of cure-alls . . . use only as directed. . . .

Malcolm Hatch was a determined young man. He had successfully made the transition from consuming the smoke of two and a half packets of cigarettes to taking up the pipe. Unfortunately, the amount of tobacco consumed in his wooden bowl had risen to the point where he felt he had gained nothing as a result. Thus, on that September afternoon when he stood across the counter of the small tobacconist's shop, he emphasized that he was not interested in anything with a gimmick. Purely and simply, he wanted to quit smoking.

The tobacconist brought out a number of items—liquids and powders, pills of various sorts which for the most part worked on the smoker's senses of taste and smell. But Malcolm was not interested. He had known too many people who had tried such preparations for a time, then simply stopped using them, their level of tobacco consumption again rising to where it had been. "You have nothing else?" Malcolm insisted.

The store proprietor looked at his customer with a strange intensity. Yes, there was something else . . . something from the rear of his shop. If the gentleman would kindly wait for just a moment . . . Malcolm waited, and soon he was looking down at a small tobacco tin. There was no label on the tin, just the single word VALEFAR. A brand name? Malcolm asked, adding the second question regarding the manufacturer. The store owner said that he himself made the preparation. As for the name, it was that of one of the demons from Hell.

Odd name for a product, Malcolm thought, but he was more interested in how the dark rich powder in the tin was to be used. "You place a small amount of it in your pipe just before you light it. This much only," the tobacconist said. First Malcolm was to load his pipe with ordinary tobacco, then just a pinch of the black powder at the top of the bowl. The price was most reasonable. But how did the powder work? Malcolm wanted to know. Again the tobacconist looked at Malcolm with that intense, strangely piercing look. As if wondering whether he might tell his customer the truth, Malcolm thought. "It works," the man said finally. Then he added that he'd developed the powder for another purpose, one which had nothing at all to do with curing a smoking

32

habit—"but its effects," he said, "are such to accomplish that as well. Repeated use and within a month's time you will no longer wish to smoke. But remember . . . no more than just a pinch!"

No sooner was Malcolm outside of the store when he loaded his briar pipe with his favorite brand of tobacco. He added just a bit of the black powder and struck a match. As the flame touched the top of the bowl, a stench—something like sulfur—poured through Malcolm's nostrils. But there was more. Before his eyes the air seemed to move, to rearrange itself. Something which was dark green in color, something with matted hair and three bulbous eyes . . . and yellow teeth surrounding a mouth which seemed to breathe fire. . . .

Malcolm Hatch screamed, the pipe dropping from his open mouth. Shaking his head, he found that the vision was gone, the day was still bright—and there on the sidewalk was his pipe, broken in two pieces at the stem. The first test of the powder had its results, he thought to himself.

As did the times which followed, these experiments made in the comfort of Malcolm's own apartment. Each time, the horrible vision would appear along with the sulfur smell. Each time his cry would expel the pipe from his mouth, not however breaking the instrument as before. And yet, as effective as the black powder seemed to be, Malcolm was not satisfied. In spite of the fact that he had taken no inhale of tobacco smoke in all his attempts, the fact was that he still wanted that smoke—he craved it.

He had his ideas about what the stuff was. Some kind of hallucinatory drug, like LSD or something like that, one which threw a real scare into the person who inhaled its fumes after touching a match to the powder. It had worked, yes, but what really was required was to scare him from wanting to light that pipe again. A larger dose, perhaps. . . .

He recalled the tobacconist's warning, of course, but thought that the warning had been given only to make sure that no one with a weak heart tried to frighten himself too much. Well, Malcolm didn't have a weak heart, and then too he knew what the stuff really was. Thus it was that perhaps he overdid the additional amount of the powder he placed into the wooden bowl. Making sure that he was seated comfortably, he struck the match and brought it closer—

The flash within the room was as if lightning had struck, the sulfuric stench burning Malcolm's nostrils as if he were inhaling a real fire. And the thing congealing in the waves of air around him. . . . It was the same beast with the horrible smell and terrifying face as before. As it came closer, Malcolm shrank back into his chair, vowing never again to use so much of the stuff. Hallucination or not, this really was frightening.

It was when the dark green something placed a hairy claw on Malcolm's trembling arm that he knew. His cry was short since Valefar, having been called from the beyond for just a little while, was in a hurry to feed. . . .

Ah, I see you smoke a pipe. Please, in the humidor on the table you'll find something I think you'll agree is quite different. I have this tobacconist friend who is an expert at delicate blends. True, he dabbles in black magic, but he keeps his two vocations completely separate for the most part.

CARAFE OF A CORPSE

The story of Durwood Beech

In order for any large organization to run smoothly there must be both leaders and followers. The pity is that, often, a follower such as Durwood Beech, even though he has neither the talent nor the wish to put in the long hours of toil necessary to succeed as a leader, still aspires to that success. It can lead to all sorts of unpleasantries . . . even death. Such was the case with Durwood Beech.

It was not so much Mr. Mulgrave's job that Durwood Beech wanted. It was what went with the job. The pretty secretary, the office with its sofa and chairs of leather and old wood, and wide expanse of antique desk, the lush deep purple carpet . . . the *things,* in other words, which would accrue to Durwood Beech if it were he and not Mr. Mulgrave who held the high-sounding title of general manager. Perhaps it was the silver carafe, though, which came to symbolize for Durwood all which he was not and all which his superior was.

It was a lovely thing. Old, yes, but carefully polished so that each time Durwood was summoned into Mr. Mulgrave's presence, the light from its bright surface immediately brought the carafe to Durwood's immediate and rapt attention. Many times he found himself staring at it—there on the corner of the baroque credenza of dark wood behind Mr. Mulgrave's desk, there on its silver tray, surrounded by four water glasses, each of which was ready to take into itself the lovely cool water which was protected within the smooth, sleek-lined silver carafe. And, thinking of what the water poured from such a device might taste like, often Durwood would be brought abruptly back to more mundane things by a sharp suggestion from his superior that he was not paying attention to what was being discussed.

Meekly Durwood would apologize, but once back into his little office, that of the administrative assistant to the general manager, an office which contained meager furniture and a dull brown plastic carafe from which Durwood never drank, Durwood would smile. For, day by day, the plot he was hatching was nearing completion. For, day by day, Durwood was doing things to the company records— things which, when revealed, would show Mr. Mulgrave to be at the very least a most incompetent steward of company property and which might even hint that the general manager had been feathering his own nest from what rightfully might have been ex-

36

pected to line the company coffers. Carefully, slowly, did Durwood Beech plot. Then he struck. A single telephone call to Chicago headquarters, a mention of an uncovered "irregularity," brought an executive vice-president to Mr. Mulgrave's office two days later. With the powerful company official came a team of auditors. They were all very efficient. In three hours they had enough to confront the general manager with what they called a number of "serious discrepancies." Further investigation, to take place the following morning, would complete their findings. In the meantime, would Mr. Mulgrave mind terribly if the office keys were kept by the executive vice-president?

What went on in Mr. Mulgrave's mind—well, one can only guess. As for Durwood Beech, already he was rubbing his hands together, anticipating the feel of Mulgrave's chair, inhaling a thick cigar behind that wide desk. For he felt that once the hated Mulgrave was deposed, the despot's throne would be given to the faithful servant. And he was right. The executive vice-president, mistaking the gleam of greed in Durwood's eyes for a gleam of intelligence, did in fact promote the "loyal" employee to the position of general manager. The very next morning, it was. The morning they found Mr. Mulgrave dead in his office chair.

He evidently had another set of keys. Also evidently—and this evidence was furnished by the police—he had poisoned himself. There was enough arsenic in the water in the silver carafe to kill *three* men. Durwood was not acting when he said he was shocked. He'd not expected his little ruse to end this way. He'd hoped only for Mulgrave's removal. But . . . inwardly he could not help smiling. Certainly Mulgrave had been removed, hadn't he? Therefore, once the offer came from the executive vice-president, he felt there was absolutely no reason for him to wait to take up his new quarters. Out of respect for the dead, however, he did wait until Mr. Mulgrave's body was removed. It was as he was getting adjusted to his swivel chair that he noticed that something was missing. The carafe! It was gone. Of course, the police would have taken it for—ah, but no, they hadn't. Mulgrave's secretary—no, now she was Durwood's secretary—explained that all the police wanted was what was inside the silver container. They were efficient, the police, having already noted for the record that the only fingerprints on the shiny surface were those of the dead man's. She, in fact, was just engaged in washing it thoroughly.

"You'll not want it in the office," the secretary said.

"*Not* want it?" Durwood laughed. "Of course I want it." He then directed her to be very sure that it was *very* clean . . . and to fill it with cold water. He felt a bit thirsty.

The girl did as she was told, not bothering to hide the look of distaste she held for the new general manager as she placed the filled carafe on its tray and then left, closing the door behind her. As for the new general manager, he was swift in filling a tumbler full of water which sparkled almost as much as the silver from which it came. He lifted the glass high, his toast a silent one, but one which was in its very gesture the height of triumph. Then he drank . . . in one gulp he emptied the tumbler. He gagged a bit . . . cried out . . . choked . . . coughed . . . and seemed to be trying to swim on the plush purple carpet.

According to the police, there was nothing unusual about the water in the carafe. But within Durwood Beech there was a good deal of arsenic—"enough to kill *three* men," the medical examiner said. . . .

The story is true. Don't ask me *how*. It is true even

though there may be no explanation. Unless . . . well, Mr. Mulgrave *was* a leader, after all . . . and Durwood Beech a follower. . . .

THE FLICKERING CANDLES

The story of Alma and Eldon Glade

Parties. They can be such crushing bores. The outcome of a gathering of people depends a bit, I suppose, upon the frame of mind of those who attend, but for the most part it is the ingenuity of the host or hostess which really makes the event. Or is that really so? Let us consider the party to which Alma and Eldon Glade were invited. Their hosts had been doing the same sort of thing year after year . . . frighteningly so. And yet it was clearly a *howling* party, mark my word. . . .

The Glades had transferred from Atlanta to a small sales district which had some very small towns, some of which had very curious names. Such as the village of Remorse, in which our story takes place. They were both in their late twenties, the Glades were, and they had found Atlanta a bustling place. Now, however, the town in which they lived was so dreary that Alma accompanied her husband on his sales tours through his district, the travel being the only diversion the poor girl could get. It was in Remorse that she received a bit more diversion than she—or Eldon—had bargained for.

The inn was old, dusty, and had about it the musty smell of decay. It was not much more than ten in the evening, but there being little else to do, the Glades decided that they would turn in early. Then the soft knock came upon the door. It was the landlady. She wanted to invite the two guests, the only guests in the inn, to Clarisse's birthday party. Little Clarisse would be so happy, the middle-aged woman said. Alma and Eldon looked at each other and sighed. Neither was tired, and if it would make some little girl happy . . .

When they arrived downstairs, they found the dining-room table set for five. The landlady and her husband insisted the guests sit to the right and to the left of Clarisse's empty place. As the Glades and the landlady's husband sat down, the landlady herself shuffled about. First she brought out the cake, then she turned out the lights, and then, sitting down, she began to light each of the candles on the cake—with a pale, cracked yellow tallow that looked as old as the hills surrounding the small village of Remorse. It was then that Alma asked about Clarisse. Where was the dear little girl? "Soon," the landlady replied as she continued lighting the candles, and now both Alma and Eldon realized that there were quite a number of the flaming columns of wax upon the top of the cake. "Little" Clarisse certainly was no child, not by the count of them, no indeed. There were at least twenty—no, thirty . . . forty . . . and the tallow still was moving to wicks still darkened.

"Clarisse so loves the candles!" the landlady said. The husband chuckled to himself, and the young couple began to feel somewhat uneasy. It was not just that a sudden wind had begun to moan outside the window behind the chair which had been reserved for the guest of honor. It was partly the fact that both Alma and Eldon still were counting the candles on that cake. Both of them had passed the ninety mark. "A hundred!" Alma gasped as she reached that number. The landlady cackled. "A hundred is not but half of them!" she said. And then the moaning wind began to intensify.

"Hurry!" the husband urged, and the landlady hurried, sighing with relief when the very last candle was lighted. Neither of the Glades had completed the count when it happened. There was a crashing of glass, the cold wind from outside now entered the room—which was plunged into darkness as the gust of air, with a dreadful sound, put out each and every one of the candles which had been in flame. In the pale of the moonlight Alma and Eldon could see the smoke wisp and curl upward from the top of the cake . . . wisp and curl and turn and . . . and then at the very top of the column of smoke there was a face. White . . . pale . . . with hollowed eyes . . . and skin which looked as if it had been deep in its grave for a long, long time.

"Happy birthday, Clarisse!" the landlady and her husband said joyously. The woman looked at the Glades. "Aren't you going to wish the dear girl happy birthday?"

But, alas, the Glades did not think to do so. They were too busy screaming. . . .

43

Parties? Ah yes, they really know how to throw a party in Remorse. . . .

THERE'S SOMETHING IN THE SOUP

The story of the Rajah Bersiong

I always find it amusing when I hear well-to-do people complaining about what they call the "servant
problem." I frequently am reminded of a saying they
have on the Malay Peninsula which translates "Don't
bleed the cook." The saying is used when one member of the household is cautioning another not to insist upon a certain dish prepared for a certain meal,
and at first foreigners do not make the connection
between the meaning of the warning and the words of
its content. Not until they hear the story behind the
saying, the true story of a local Malay ruler who came
to be known as the *Rajah Bersiong* . . . Rajah with
fangs. As we have our dinner, I shall tell you the
tale. . . .

It happened more than five hundred years ago in
the vicinity of what is now known as Kedah. The rich
ruler of the area was a proud man, proud of his

45

military might, his immense wealth, his palace with its immense and finely woven tapestries, his handsome looks, his wives and his children, the fine marriages he had arranged for his sons and daughters. Of all these things was the Rajah proud, but he took perhaps his greatest delight in the culinary delights with which he continually surprised his guests at table. For the Rajah had, within his kitchen retinue, an old man who, based upon the testimony of many of the nobility as well as the testimony of his own palate, was the finest cook in that part of the country, and perhaps in any part of the East. And so it was that the Rajah never dictated to the kitchen as to what was to be served—never. While the number of people to be fed and their relative importance always was communicated to the august preparer of the meals, always the decision regarding what to serve and how was left to the cook himself.

Until that one night . . .

It was to be a special soup, something the cook never had prepared before. The basic ingredients of the new effort are unknown today, because whenever the old cook created something new, he allowed no one else in the kitchen with him. Whatever those ingredients were, however, this much is known: One of the elements to be stirred into the broth required some extra fine chopping. And it was while performing this operation that the old cook inadvertently placed his left index finger just a bit too close to the flashing blade of his chopping knife. It was a reflexive motion that caused the painful hand to jerk up from the cutting board and stop at a point directly over the cooking pot of boiling broth. And into the pot something fell. Three drops of blood.

At first the cook thought his effort had been ruined, and he was considering whether he should begin the entire process again. But it was growing close to the time when the Rajah and his guests would be sitting down to eat. The cook's mind frantically thought of alternatives which he could hurriedly prepare, but at last he decided that there was nothing he could do. Nothing except to serve the tainted soup as it was. He added the final ingredients, then tasted it. He was satisfied that no one would suspect that there was something in his creation which should not be there.

How terrifyingly wrong he was! And how horrified he became when, the next day, the Rajah himself came into the kitchen. He had loved the soup, he said. He had tasted nothing like it—ever. So much did he crave the delicacy that he wanted more this evening. And then he added two specific instructions. The first was that although the same amount of the soup was to be prepared, it was to be served to himself alone, to consume within his own apartment. The second instruction was that more of the special ingredient should be added.

The cook was shocked. "Special ingredient?" he asked.

"Yes," the Rajah replied, wetting his lips. "Whatever it is, you know the element I mean. Is that not true?"

The Rajah's eyes held the look of ice in them. The poor cook, knowing well that the penalty for displeasing his employer was an agonizing torture and a merciless death, could not but admit that he knew the special ingredient of which the Rajah spoke, the ingredient of which he himself dared not to speak. And so that night he followed his instructions, cutting gently into his finger and adding his blood to the broth—but this time six drops—and then carrying the bowl through the halls of the palace to the darkened apartment of the Rajah.

The next day the ruler again visited his kitchen. The cook dreaded hearing the words of his master, yet he knew what they would be. The soup was even more delicious than before. It obviously was the effect of that special something, thus its quantity again was to be increased.

And so it went for more than a full cycle of the moon. Night after night the old cook prepared the same meal for his master, night after night adding increased amounts of his own blood into the broth, and night after night carrying his preparation to the darkened rooms of the Rajah. And then one morning word came from the servants' quarters that the old cook was dead. The entire household had recognized that he had become quite pale as of late, and his final end had not gone unanticipated. Thus it was with some alarm that the household heard their master scream hysterically at the news. And then came the further news that he had shut himself up into his rooms with the order that none should enter—none except those bringing his meals to him at the appointed time of day.

It was not until three days thereafter that the whispers among the servants came to the ears of the eldest of the Rajah's daughters, who with her husband was visiting her father's palace. Two young serving girls were nowhere to be found within the palatial halls. Both of them had been those assigned to bring to the cloistered Rajah his evening meals on the two previous days. The daughter was incensed at the veiled accusation against her father. She instructed the kitchen that, on this night, she herself would bring the tray to the ruler. And thus it was that she did so, knocking gently upon his door at the appointed time, hearing his voice—but a strange voice it seemed—instructing her to enter, and then entering.

Her father stood in a dark corner of the room, his back to the door. "Enter, please," he said, indicating a table near where he stood as the place the tray should be deposited. It was not until the girl had done as she was directed that her father turned. She screamed with all her strength as he stepped from the shadows and she saw his face . . . the wild black hair . . . the sharp red-stained fangs. . . .

Fortunately for the girl, her husband had not felt comfortable allowing her to complete her mission by herself. Unknown to her he had followed. And now it was his sword which flashed and took from the Rajah's shoulders in one sweep the horrible monster-head. It rolled to a high lacquered cabinet which, when opened, was found to contain the bodies of the two servant girls . . . their blood-drained bodies.

Ah! A hideous story, I admit . . . not one which perhaps should be told over dinner. And I have been remiss on not mentioning the excellence of your salad, my dear. The dressing, especially. There is something . . . well, *different* about it.

DON'T KILL THE LITTLE LAMB

The story of the Fletcher family

I see the way your child plays with his pet. A warm, homey scene, isn't it? And it teaches the child affection as well as a sense of responsibility, true? Of course, there might be such a thing as a child becoming a little too attached to an animal—yes, there might be. The Fletcher family just might be a case in point. . . .

The Fletcher farm was located in New Hampshire, in a rather isolated area of that state. Gareth, age eight, and Libby, age six, had to walk for more than forty-five minutes to get to school. That was, of course, when they walked fast and didn't linger along the way. The point was that recently their parents had been getting reports from the school that the children were showing up very late, and there were one or two days when they did not come to school at all, days when there was no excuse to be made such as sickness. The parents had a rather firm idea of what

51

was behind it all. It was the black lamb.

Mr. and Mrs. Fletcher had given it to the children as a pet. In the beginning it had been an extremely sickly creature, but Gareth and Libby cared for it so well that its black coat turned full and its overall energy level surpassed the norm for such animals at its age. Yet there was a disturbing quality about the little creature. Not only did Mr. and Mrs. Fletcher feel, well, *uncomfortable* about the black lamb, but the other animals on the farm seemed to shun it. The two dogs, for example, would go nowhere near the lamb, and whenever it came near one of them, the dog would promptly disappear. The children, however, loved their little black lamb and wanted it to go with them everywhere, even to school. The famous nursery rhyme to the contrary, schools are no place for little lambs, regardless of how much the children might enjoy their presence, so the practice was put to a halt. That was, of course, the time that Gareth and Libby began to attend classes with less regularity than before.

The decision was a difficult one, but it had to be made. Mr. Fletcher announced it gravely: the lamb had to go. There were tears and pleadings, but both parents stood firm. Before the end of the week, the lamb would be gone from the farm. It was then that Gareth told his father that several times they had been asked by an old woman if they wanted to sell their pet and, since she had said that they could visit the animal at her place, this might be a solution. Mr. Fletcher did not comment at that point, but the next day, when a thin old crone presented herself at their door, he decided it might well provide the best solution. For one thing, she lived quite far from the Fletcher farm, far enough that the children would soon tire of the long walk to see their former pet. He was sure of it.

But a week after the lamb had been sold, he was less sure. It was a dark night in October when Mrs. Fletcher reported that the children's beds were empty, and that earlier she had heard them whispering about the lamb. She definitely had heard the word *party* mentioned. So it was that the Fletchers drove their truck to the place where the old woman lived. The house itself was dilapidated and dark, but from the barn there appeared to be some light . . . and the sound of voices singing softly. A strange song it was and, as Mr. and Mrs. Fletcher came nearer, the sound of the melody, somewhat off key, and the strange foreign words chilled them to the marrow of their bones. But it was not until they stepped up to the open door that icy hands of fear clutched their hearts.

Most of the people inside were dressed in long black robes, all but three of them. The old woman, standing by what looked to be an altar of some kind, wore a white flowing gown. The two Fletcher children wore their normal clothing as they stood, one on each side of the altar. Upon the altar was the black lamb which, suddenly now, began bleating. The singing abruptly stopped and all eyes turned toward the entrance and to the two intruders. It was little Libby who spoke first:

"Daddy, Mommy! They want to kill our little lamb. They say they have to for their—"

She couldn't think of the word. "Ceremony," Gareth supplied. Then he added. "They said that they must kill our lamb—unless we find them a substitute . . . something for them to kill. We couldn't think of any substitute . . . not until now. . . ."

It took a moment before Mr. and Mrs. Fletcher grasped the boy's meaning. By that time they themselves were being grasped, by several pairs of strong hands . . . hands which now were shoving them forward . . . toward the altar. They saw the long sharp

53

knife on the altar then, just as Gareth said, with a childish smile, "We love our lamb, Father . . . we want him with us . . . always. . . ."

A rather disquieting tale, don't you think? But look there—when you just now reprimanded your child's pet for chewing on the carpet—did you see how your child reacted . . . the look in his eyes? . . .

CHAINS

The story of Constable Rufus Steed

You can't judge a book by its cover. How often we've all heard that sage old proverb, one in which Constable Rufus Steed firmly believed. He believed it right up till the grisly end, when the truth of the proverb was put to a rather crucial test. . . .

The little English hamlet in which Rufus Steed was constable was used to quiet times. But when the horrible murders took place it was anything but quiet—not in the daylight hours, that is. At night, all was quiet as death itself. The door of every house was locked up tight. The only sound was that of some lonely dog . . . or wolf. Indeed, the daytime noise the citizenry made, either in the hamlet's single pub or in Constable Steed's office, had much to do with wolves. Because, you see, the first two murders occurred on the first nights of the full moon. Both victims were young damsels and their throats had been torn out . . . as if by the fangs of some . . . wolf.

"A werewolf!" was the cry raised on the morning of the third day, but the cry was not directed at something whose daylight whereabouts and identity were unknown. No, all accusatory eyes lifted to the high hill overlooking the hamlet, and to the dark-walled baronial manor which loomed upward from the heights.

Constable Steed did not have to be told why that was the place where suspicion rested. Less than a week previous, young Hilliard Drew had returned from many years in London. A nice, clean young man, Hilliard Drew seemed, and it was not himself whom the people of the hamlet suspected. No, it was his older brother Giles, whom Hilliard had brought back with him. . . . Giles, whose very face was a study of twisted evil, whose body was bent over forward as if his sins weighed down his stooping shoulders, whose cold, clouded right eye looked as if transfixed on the sight of Hell itself. But it was not the way Giles looked, not that alone, which struck terror in the hearts of the people. It was also the fact that, prior to the brothers' return, Giles had been cloistered in a sanitarium. For a few days after their taking up the old family residence, conversation in the hamlet expressed real pity for young Mr. Hilliard—such a pity that his work or his studies or whatever he was up to in London had to be interrupted so that he could care, bless him, for his demented brother.

And then came the murders. So it was that, on the day after the second of the two deaths, Constable Steed visited Drew Manor. He was graciously received by young Hilliard Drew who, upon learning of the two poor girls' end, expressed his view that he thought it was shocking, "really shocking." But it was when the constable inquired after Mr. Giles that the younger brother looked really disturbed. "Not at all well, not at all," Hilliard Drew said. The constable said that he'd like to question both of the brothers, to find out whether either had heard or seen anything strange in the past two nights. He also mentioned that there was talk of a werewolf in connection with the crimes.

"A werewolf," Hilliard Drew said heavily. "They do exist, you know. I have no idea whether one is responsible for the unfortunate occurrences you speak of, but they do exist. Very sad, very. They can't help themselves, it's a fact." As to whether he had heard or seen anything, he replied that he certainly had not, and, as for "poor Giles—no, he wouldn't have, either." It was, Hilliard added firmly, quite impossible for Giles to be questioned.

Constable Steed left the house shortly thereafter, but he reflected that *impossible* was a word he didn't like to use with regard to his business. Thus it was shortly after dark when the constable, using an ill-got device often used by professional burglars, reentered Drew Manor. He had barely closed the door silently behind him when he hastily withdrew into a shadowed corner, just barely making it in time. Coming through the doorway which, from the look of it, led down somewhere below the main floor of the manor, was Hilliard Drew, a flashlight in his hand. Constable Steed waited until the light and the footfalls faded, then he flicked on his own flashlight and moved to the doorway. Down and down the stone stairs he went, careful to make no noise whatever. When he reached the bottom—

It was a cell, just like you'd find in any jail, except that the steel was rustier and the general condition of the place was filthy. Behind the barred door was the hideous form of Giles Drew. Seeing the flashlight, the misshapen man acted as if he wanted to speak, but all that came out was a croaking noise. The creature *could not* speak! Yet the look on the man's face could

57

not be mistaken. That—and the way his arms extended toward the cell door. . . . It was an act of supplication. To be released from the cell, and from the chains which, the constable now realized, were fastened to his wrists. With a swift movement, Constable Steed had his service revolver in his hand, cocked and pointed. Then . . .

You can't judge a book by its cover, he reflected. He let the hammer move slowly forward, uncocking the pistol. "Did you kill two women?" he asked. Wildly, Giles shook his head no, then he did something else. With a single index finger, he pointed upward. Upstairs. *Hilliard!* Constable Steed accepted the accusation, he knew not why, but he knew that it fit with his own thinking. Noticing that there was light coming in from a barred window behind the chained man—moonlight, obviously—he turned off his flash and set to work on the door. When he had successfully opened that, he grasped the wrist of Giles Drew and applied himself to that lock. *If,* he thought—*if I am wrong . . .*

Giles moved not at all, not after the first lock was sprung, not after the second wristlock was released. He stood, his one good eye staring into the eyes of the constable, his mouth opening and closing until—

Until the voice of Hilliard Drew cried out. "Good God! Constable! You didn't—you couldn't have—"

He stood about fifteen feet from the open cell. Before the constable knew what had happened, the man beside him—Giles Drew—had roared like a bull and swept him aside. He seemed to leap through the open door, leap toward his younger brother like some charging beast, like . . . a wolf!

"Stand back!" the constable commanded, but no one obeyed, the deranged brother attacking Hilliard Drew as if with killer instinct. Having issued his warning, Constable Steed lifted his revolver and fired two shots—straight into the back of Giles Drew. "Stupid!" he reviled himself as he bent over the dead man. "Stupid!"

"He knew," Hilliard Drew said.

Constable Steed nodded. "Knew he was a werewolf, you mean?"

"No, Constable. He knew that *I am!*"

The good constable tried to lift his pistol to a position where it might do some good, but it was much too late. The moonlight spilling into the dungeon room gave him a quick but more than ample look at the wild face and fanged mouth which were rushing toward him. In the instant before his throat was slashed, the constable knew that there was indeed truth in that old adage and that he had been right, not wrong, about Giles.

Small consolation, don't you think?

KEEPER OF THE VAULT

The story of the Clement gang

In American criminal annals, the 1920s and 1930s are full of such bloodthirsty luminaries. Oh, the sagas, the songs that have been sung of them. There are, however, no songs, no sagas about the Clement gang. You see, they only—to use the romantic idiom—"pulled one job." And that one, well . . .

The dusty town of Huxley was the site chosen, not for any aesthetic reason to be sure, but because the bank there—on a particular Thursday night—was holding a goodly sum of payroll money. Now, other bank robbers gained fame from boldly walking into their target bank during broad daylight, but the Clement gang, in planning its first accumulation of others' funds, decided that a daylight operation offered too many dangers. Thus, they opted for the still hours of dark night. Had they *known* of course . . .

But they didn't. In fact, the four members of the

gang—Harold Clement, Will Clement, Sam Clement and a final member colorfully called Kid Blast—were quite successful in gaining entry into the interior of the bank without setting off any alarm. They also did quite well in letting themsleves into the cage just before the strong vault. The vault itself, of course, would have to be opened with a bit of noise, and that was the specialty of Kid Blast, whose expertise included the use of the several bundles of dynamite which he busily was arranging about the heavy steel door. He was, in fact, engaged in the arranging when the four members of the Clement gang discovered to their dismay that there were *five* men gathered before the vault.

The fifth man was a rather disconcerting being. It was not so much his old style of dress, but more the face of the man. His head was totally hairless, shaped much like a fleshless skull . . . his eyes seemed to be fiery torches . . . and his voice, for all its rage, sounded as if it were a booming echo coming from some bottomless pit: "You dare—you dare to think you can take *my* money?"

The three Clement brothers and Kid Blast were frozen in shock at the sight of the old man as he pointed a bony finger toward the dynamite which lay about the floor. As the four robbers followed the gesture, their eyes opened wide in horror. None of them missed the ignited, sputtering fuse as it hissed its way toward a bundle of the deadly red cylinders.

The explosion rocked the town, bringing to the scene curious but cautious townspeople, armed with rifles and shotguns. When the first group of these, approaching the bank from the rear, stepped through the rent in the wall, they affirmed that the thick vault was still intact. There were, however, parts of three men scattered ingloriously throughout the cage. The fourth man was found out in the small lobby of the bank, quite near the front door.

Harold Clement was badly burned, but it was not that which seemed to be causing the strange sounds the man was making—alternating low sobs and high-pitched cries. He was standing there, his eyes round and bulbous, focused upon the portrait on the wall, the portrait of the bank's founder who had been dead for some twenty years.

Even in life the old man's head had been shaped like a fleshless skull. . . .

PUT ON A DEADLY FACE

The story of Silas Friday

How amusing they are, those clowns in the circus, the ones with the bright and happy faces. Some of the sad-looking clowns, too, can make us smile and even laugh as they go through antics which remind us of our all-too-human frailty. But then there are those other clowns we see now and then, those with faces so sad that they appear to be the holders of some truth too terrible to speak of aloud. These clowns, regardless of their movements down in the center ring or outside of it, cause no laughs, no smiles. Only a shudder, a cold chill deep within our spines. . . .

Silas Friday was such a clown. His painted face with its down-turned eyes and so-sad mouth, its drooping nose . . . when combined with the baggy suit he wore, his entire presence was one which was disconcerting not only to the paying customers but also to other members of the circus troupe. This in itself says much, in that people who have been around circuses and carnivals usually long have gotten used to seeing odd and sometimes hideous manifestations of the human form, especially those versions of humanity which haunt the dark contrasts of shadow and light in and around the freak tents. Even so, there was hardly a member of the troupe who was not unsettled by the clown face of Silas Friday.

Silas Friday himself had no explanation for the effect he caused. He knew that there were sad clowns and happy clowns, he knew that he'd always been a sad clown, just as he knew that he could not abruptly change his makeup, his clothes, his manner of walk and thus become something other than what he was. He knew that—for a clown's costume is much more than just the simple trappings he wears under the bright lights. No. The costume and face, all of it, are an extension of *himself*. Silas Friday had never seriously thought of changing into something other than himself—not, at least, until that one Friday night.

Eddie Lot had been a clown for even more years than Silas. Eddie Lot, however, was a happy clown. His suit was stuffed full to almost complete roundness, his waddle brought happy cheers from children and adults alike, but it was his facial makeup which was the main cause of the happiness he spread. He once told Silas, "You can't look at my face without at least smiling." That wasn't precisely correct, because Silas Friday didn't smile at Eddie's face. He hated it. It reminded him of his own shortcomings as a clown.

Two things happened on that special Friday. The first was the business manager's visit to Silas's tent. Because of pressure from the rest of the troupe, the manager was going to have to let Silas go. Tonight would be his last show. The second thing was Eddie

Lot's death. Natural causes, to be sure, but it got Silas thinking. Silas, you see, was the first to learn of Eddie's end. He had gone to the happy clown's tent to ask him for advice. Eddie was half into his makeup, his head resting on the dressing table. It was less than an hour from showtime.

Quickly, Silas made his decision. He did not want to touch the dead man, but there was no choice. He moved the body onto the tent floor, then he began. The round costume beside him, he stripped the rubber headpiece from the top of Eddie's skull and, sitting before the mirror, placed it upon his own. A bald white dome with strands of straw-colored hair shooting directly outward just over the ears. Silas shivered as he saw his reflection, but shook off the feeling, instead concentrating upon the paints. He worked swiftly, skillfully, having seen Eddie's laughing face with its twinkling eyes and high, upturned mouth so many times that he could have done the job in the dark. And in a way, even though the tent was brightly lighted, it felt dark here. . . .

Silas knew why. Eddie's face and costume had been a part of Eddie, and of no one else. For a clown to adopt another's costume was the highest of professional sacrilege. But, Silas told himself, again and again, *Eddie is dead . . . he won't mind.* . . . Still, though, the taking of another clown's face . . . Suddenly Silas looked behind him, down at the floor where Eddie lay. No, there was no movement. For a moment there, he'd thought he'd heard . . . soft laughter. . . .

But only one or two touches more—there! It was done, completed! And now to check carefully in the mirror, to be sure everything was exactly right. Silas chuckled at the way his mouth moved, smiling at the funny little eyes and the shaggy eyebrows above them. It was true—the face *was* funny. He laughed tentatively; then, seeing the face in the mirror laugh back, he laughed again, this time more loudly. He laughed so hard his stomach began to hurt. . . .

The hysterical sounds were over by the time the others reached the tent. Silas Friday sat back in his chair, that wide funny grin painted on his face, a face the happiness of which was marred only by the rivulets on the cheeks where tears from his eyes had spoiled the makeup. Both Silas Friday and Eddie Lot were judged to have died from heart failure, but the people of the circus knew better. One of them—the one who had been a thief of the other's face—had died a victim of his own theft.

You hear people, now and again, use the phrase, "I almost died laughing." It is not a phrase to be used lightly . . . is it?

BLOOD MONEY

The story of Uncle Lester

Come, let us look into the home of a typical Midwestern American family. A cozy house, a mother and father and a four-year-old boy whose name is Clarence. The father and mother have worked hard all their lives, and they have taught their son the value of thrift even at his early age. His piggy bank with its rattling coins is one of his proudest possessions. There is a fourth member of the family, too, but only temporarily. Uncle Lester is visiting for a time. Uncle Lester is father's older brother, quite a bit older. A genial sort of person is Uncle Lester, but he does not believe overly much in the virtues of work. Many families have counterparts of Uncle Lester who manage quite well by extended visits with softhearted relatives. Sometimes they strain the patience of the home, sometimes the very fabric of family life, but usually they are allowed to remain until someone . . . or something . . . takes a hand. Takes a hand—yes, an appropriate phrase.

Uncle Lester had traveled to many places and he had many stories to tell of his early adventures as he smoked his pipe out on the front porch. But lately mother and father were tiring of the stories and their hope was that Uncle Lester would soon make his departure. The problem was, you see, that Uncle Lester was stealing from the family. Oh, not all that much in monetary terms, to be sure; just enough to buy his tobacco. But he was taking the money from little Clarence's piggy bank.

"Pig," as the bank was called, was a large metal container which father had made himself from a metal container and mother had decorated to look like a pig. Ears had been fashioned from papier mache, a curled tail had been made from a wire coat hanger, and the entire device was given a coat of gleaming yellow and black spotted paint. Clarence loved Pig, not just for the sake of the money inside, but also for the "talks" they would have together. For, you see, father had constructed Pig so that at the front was a hinged jaw which was movable. Thus Clarence often could be seen working the jaw up and down during their periods of conversation. The real function of the jaw, of course, was the insertion of money—and the withdrawal of money as well. It was clear that Uncle Lester was doing a bit of withdrawing.

At first mother and father weren't eager to believe the teary-eyed boy, but they knew well that he knew precisely how many pennies, nickels, dimes, quarters and fifty-cent pieces Pig held. With too much regularity, coins of the upper values were disappearing. Father, in the hope that soon the problem and Uncle Lester would go away, began replenishing Pig's missing funds, but it was not the same—not to

Little Clarence, anyway. He decided he would catch Uncle Lester in the act. So night after night, he lay in his upstairs bed, pretending to be asleep, hoping . . . waiting . . . and then, of course, falling asleep anyway, dreaming hateful dreams of what he would do to his uncle when the thief was caught.

He was in the midst of such a dream when the agonized cry brought him to a sitting position. The room was dark, but a bit of moonlight that came through the window showed him that there was someone else in the room . . . over by where Pig normally sat on the bureau. Again the cry sounded—loud and horrible. Clarence was frightened then, and he started to run from the room. But Uncle Lester's scream stopped him. "Help me! Your parents are out—help me!" And then Clarence turned on the light. When he saw what there was to see, he no longer was frightened. He just sat on the edge of the bed and, his eyes narrowing to cold black dots, he watched.

When mother and father came home, they found Uncle Lester lying halfway down the stairs. Very dead, of course, after losing all that blood, but there were two questions for which satisfactory answers never were found. One . . . what had caused that look of horror which had frozen itself onto Uncle Lester's face? Two . . . what had happened to Uncle Lester's right hand, which had been severed off at a point just below the wrist? True, little Clarence had been home at the time, but he had been asleep when he heard Uncle Lester call for help, he said. Obviously the boy wasn't going to be of very much help, so mother and father and the police said he could run along. He did, to the outside water faucet. There he sat down and took all his money from Pig's stomach. The coins . . . and Pig's insides as well . . . had to be washed

71

thoroughly. Everything was so . . . messy. . . .

A disturbing tale? Oh, I don't know . . . unless there's a piggy bank in your house . . . and you're short just a couple of coins. . . .

THE FISHMONGER

The story of Albert Able

In many lands at many times the belief has been that if you eat the flesh of another . . . or drink his blood . . . you acquire his power. One can scoff at such beliefs as being little more than primitive superstition. I think, for example, that Albert Able might have done so . . . before he began his strange diet of a certain peculiar sort of seafood. . . .

The day it all began Albert Able was miserable. Not only was the day itself rather gloomy for spring in San Francisco, but it was the day prior to his first important case in court, and the lawyer who was to be his opposition was well known as a sharp-thinking master of verbal battle who never had lost in courtroom conflict. Albert had all his facts, knew that by all rights he *should* win the case, but deep within him he knew that against such formidable opposition as old Geddry he didn't stand much of a chance. Such were his thoughts as he walked along the wharf, thoughts of gloom so heavy that it took a bit of time for him to realize that the grinning man with the white apron standing outside the small store was speaking to him. When he understood what the man was saying, he shook his head, first at the man himself, then at the four red letters on the glass window: FISH.

But the man in the white apron insisted that Albert Able come inside and have at least a look, that among the fish he had in his cases there was one which was very special, one he was sure was just the thing which Albert required. Albert nodded absentmindedly and, rather than offend the fish seller, followed him inside the store and to the cases. He would look, then say something about not caring for fish, then he would leave. That was his intention, but when he saw the particular fish the man in the apron took from the case and lay on the counter, he suddenly was more than interested.

"What kind of fish is that?" he asked warily, but the fish seller merely smiled. "A special fish," he replied. "One that, if eaten tonight, should give you a degree of success . . . for tomorrow." It was, Albert Able decided, an uncanny coincidence. The man's words . . . and this fish, the features of which about the head resembled a man's features. Not those of just any man, but those of . . . old Geddry. Hastily, Albert Able paid the price for the fish—a small price comparable to those in the display case which advertised the prices of other types of food from the sea. Just as hastily he went to his apartment and cleaned and cooked the fish he had bought. Its taste was nothing spectacular, but he ate all of it. He felt no different afterward.

But the next day in court, Albert Able trampled all

over old Geddry. It was as if the seasoned lawyer had forgotten every point of law he'd ever known. His eyes looked dull, his speech was slow, his manner of handling the entire case was, in a word, bumbling. And late that afternoon Albert went back to the wharf to the fish seller's shop. The man in the white apron ignored Albert's questions by repeatedly asking him if he enjoyed the fish he had purchased the previous day. Finally Albert shouted. "Yes!" Then, before he could say anything more, he was looking at another fish. This one, too, had humanlike features, but Albert didn't recognize them. Yet he bought this special fish—at a price slightly higher than the other had cost—and that evening it was the mainstay of his dinner meal. It was more than a week later when Albert met the man whose features matched those of the fish. He was supposedly a very talented New York lawyer who had been flown in to handle the court case against another of Albert's clients. His talents, whatever they were, were not apparent in the courtroom. Albert Able, to the delight of his client, made the New Yorker look like a country bumpkin fresh out of law school.

It took no time at all for Albert's clientele to grow—in terms of number and of influence and wealth. Preparatory to each courtroom confrontation, from each of which he emerged the clear victor, he would pay a visit to the seller of special fish. Each time the price went up, but not considerably, and after all Albert Able was fast becoming a man of means who could afford to spend a bit on the delights of the stomach. So he did not balk at the prices, not until that fateful day when the price quoted was no less than five thousand dollars! Albert gaped at the fish seller, hardly believing his ears. Then he stepped back from his counter and his face took on his courtroom demeanor. No, he would not pay the price. As a matter of fact, he really didn't believe that he required the services of the fish seller any longer. Really, it had been nothing more than some sort of hallucination anyway—yes, that was it. Really, it had been Albert's talents alone which had given him his successes.

The man in the white apron nodded and smiled at Albert's little speech. He said that he understood fully and that, if such was the gentleman's decision, so be it. But there was one thing. Without Albert's support, he'd have to find another customer. It might not be too hard to do that, considering—well, *this* special item he had for sale.

It took only a moment for the gasping Albert Able to decide. He took the original fish offered, writing out a hasty check for five thousand dollars. He also took the second, the one which the fish seller gave him for nothing, the one which made Albert realize that he'd be coming here again and again . . . the one with Albert's own face. . . .

I think of Albert Able often . . . as often as I am served fish. His story, I find, is . . . well . . . food for thought. . . .

DARK SECRET

The story of the Knights of Hell

There are places in this world where darkness rules undisputed, places where the light of the sun is an unwelcome foreigner, places such as the catacombs under ancient cities and the tombs of the dead, or the depths of steaming jungles closed from light by thick growths above. . . . To places such as these the dwellers of the Dark are drawn, for it is there they can adapt best, they can dwell without distraction . . . and grow. . . . But there is darkness among man's civilized dwellings as well, and sometimes when conditions are right—when the dark, the dank, the fetid and the foul are found in the precise measures—the trappings of modern civilization are but a veneer, a mask which for a time hides the existence of something primeval . . . a creeping something. . . .

The Knights of Hell ranged in age from twelve to seventeen, but among the gangs of the streets in

Spanish Harlem they were known for their swift brand of brutal justice which involved discriminate use of flesh-rending blades, bone-crushing pipes, face-maiming chains and other implements of similar delicacy. In the two-block tenement area where the Knights held sway, young boys between the ages of twelve and seventeen found it wise at least to render due obedience to the gang; the ideal, of course, was to be an actual member. But membership was not all that freely bestowed. One had to be invited. Big Juan was invited, but he turned the offer down. That was the beginning of the end for the Knights of Hell.

It was a thing unheard of—turning down membership. Big Juan himself was not considered to be all that valuable to the gang. He was in fact considered to be quite stupid for a boy of thirteen. Slow in speech, slow in movement, he was assessed to have the mental power of a lad half of his age. The only assets he offered were his size and his strength, both of which were considerable. For, stupid as he might be, no one had quite enough nerve to pick on Big Juan—certainly not on a one-to-one basis. His explanation for not wishing to join the gang was as unnerving as the refusal itself. The Knights of Hell had meetings in the late afternoon, he said. He was busy in the late afternoon, and that was that.

Except, of course, that it wasn't. What was Big Juan up to? The question became the main topic of conversation among the Knights. There were some who suspected that he had a girl friend, but most agreed that no girl would bother with the big hulking idiot. There were others who thought that he might have taken up with a rival gang, but that too seemed unlikely. The question, however, had to be resolved. A watch therefore would be kept on Big Juan and his movements duly reported.

It was not long before the reports were assessed.

Every day at about four in the afternoon, Big Juan went to an area which contained a block of condemned buildings. He would enter one building in particular and stay there, sometimes till six. Then he would go home. The secret, obviously, was in that building. And so it was that on one particular Tuesday, the Knights of Hell watched as Big Juan entered the cankerous shell of what had once been an apartment house. Silently they followed, listening in the darkness. Ah! There was a basement—see the stairs there! And yes—they could hear Big Juan down there, whisperng to someone. Someone was living here perhaps, or perhaps the someone had slipped in earlier, through another way. In any case, the Knights soon would know.

"Juan!" they called out. "We're coming down!"

"No!" Big Juan shouted back. "Wait!" And with speed no one had ever seen before, the large boy came bounding up the stairs. "No—please! You cannot go down there!"

But of course there was no way Big Juan was going to stop them. His brute force, even he realized, was no match for the sharp knives and razors, the chains and bludgeons, and—yes—the small, pearl-handled pistol which one of the Knights now was aiming directly at Big Juan's chest. "We will go down, Juan," the leader said. "We will go down and we will see."

They did. From upstairs Big Juan heard it all. The shouts, the screams, the firing of two shots from the small pearl-handled pistol, and then silence. He went down the stairs sobbing, knowing full well what he would see at the bottom, in the dark, cold cellar. The smell of death was everywhere. All the boys who perhaps were not his friends but were not his enemies, either. But they weren't the important thing. His face wet with tears, he called out a name in a whisper, and then called out the same name louder. Finally he shouted the name, a strange name that was not English and wasn't Spanish, a name that the Thing had told him. It was when the echo of his own voice came back into his brain that Big Juan knew. The Thing which was his friend was gone. But perhaps . . . yes, perhaps . . . perhaps it would come back . . . after a time, when it knew only Juan was here.

And so Big Juan sat down in the cold dark cellar. He sat down among the remains of the Knights of Hell . . . to wait for a friend. . . .

A sad ending? Perhaps so, but Juan's despair need not be yours. No, not if in your neighborhood there is a damp place which always is shrouded in darkness. . . . Why not visit there some night? You may meet a friend . . . a lifelong friend. . . .

THE MASKED DOLLS

The story of Stanton Fry

Do you believe in the powers of voodoo? There are
many, many people who do, you know. Ah yes, it is
quite true that the majority of these believers are not
what you might call *educated* people, and so I suppose that you, with your superior knowledge, might
have a case for saying that voodoo—and the effects
which have been ascribed to it—well, they're not
much more than silly superstition. Stanton Fry and
his friends would have agreed with you completely,
you know. But let us consider what happened to Stanton Fry, shall we?

A wealthy young man was Stanton Fry. Excellent
Bostonian family, Harvard educated, thinking in fact
of running for a Congressional seat. His yacht in the
summers always was a setting for what we have come
to call the "beautiful people." This particular sum-
mer the yacht and its people were meandering about

the Caribbean. It was, of course, in Haiti that the subject of voodoo came to the forefront of the group's conversation.

Stanton Fry was a disbeliever, a scoffer, if you will. Whether or not everyone else in his entourage shared his views in reality, the fact was that all of them voiced agreement. One does not, after all, purposely challenge the strongly felt views of one's host, especially when that host had the power of wealth and family behind him. However, even though there were no dissenters with regard to his stated views, Stanton Fry insisted upon demonstrating the correctness of those views. Besides, the group was running just a bit dry on new entertainment ideas.

It was arranged, through a local official—who, it must be said, did his best to warn against the whole thing—that an accepted practitioner of the voodoo art put on a show aboard the yacht. During the afternoon prior to the evening selected, a small rowboat delivered an old white-haired black man who, when he confronted Stanton Fry, said that he had been asked to perform before Mr. Fry and his friends. He wished to know exactly what kind of performance was requested. Stanton Fry, his eyes twinkling, responded, "Proof." He then elaborated. "Whatever you do tonight, everyone on board will be looking for your tricks. We'll find them, believe me. You're supposed to be an expert—see if you can fool us!"

The black man replied that voodoo did not attempt to fool anyone, that it was nothing to laugh at, to treat lightly. Nonetheless, he would do his best to prove his powers—and the power inherent in the thing which was called voodoo.

There was a bit of drinking that night before the old man appeared, and it took Stanton Fry more than a few minutes to get his guests quiet. When he had

82

center stage, Stanton Fry introduced the old man who was going to "perform wonders before their very eyes." He laughed at his own words, then stood aside as the old man smiled at the group.

"You do not believe," he said, "but look upon these." The *these* he referred to were dolls, quite a few of them, which he took out of an old battered basket. Each of the dolls had its face hidden, a tiny scarflike cloth tied around its head. The old man handed a doll to each of the guests. The last to receive one was Stanton Fry. As the final exchange took place, the old man's eyes narrowed, then he turned again to the group as a whole. "Here," he said, "are steel pins, long and sharp. If you would know the power of voodoo, merely take a pin and pass it through the doll you hold."

Eagerly Stanton Fry's guests grabbed for the pins, holding them poised for a thrust, but none making a further move. They all understood that it was Stanton Fry's party. It was up to him to act first. With a laugh of derision Stanton Fry sent his pin into the torso of the masked doll he had been given. With echoing laughs, other pins followed into the other dolls—in their arms and legs, into their heads. It was all accomplished before the sound of the sudden shriek of horror reached the guests' ears. And by that time, it was much too late.

The silence was broken only by the dipping oars of the boat which rowed the old man toward the shoreline as the guests of Stanton Fry looked from the unmasked dolls they clutched—dolls which all wore the face of their host—to the mangled, bloodied body of Stanton Fry himself, twisted and torn on the deck of his very expensive yacht. . . .

Needless to say, that night there were those who changed their minds about the powers of voodoo.

How about you? Do you believe—oh, not just in what is known as voodoo, but in any of the Black Arts? Careful, now . . . don't answer until you're sure . . . sure that no one else is listening. . . .

THE EMPTY CLOSET

The story of Josiah Ward

Have you noticed that sometimes the most frightening occurrences take place directly as a result of someone's curiosity. "Curiosity killed the cat," we say, and we add, "Let well enough alone." Indeed, several of my tales which you have listened to already have dealt with the theme, but even if they had not, surely there are few among us who are not familiar with the tragedy which the mythical Pandora's curiosity set upon the world simply because she was curious as to what was in a closed box. And yet, we do not learn from others' examples, do we? Josiah Ward really should have known better, but . . . well, let us speak of Josiah Ward and the curiosity which killed him. . . . Or perhaps it didn't kill him. I can't really say. . . .

A young man of twenty-six was Josiah Ward when he was left, through the death of some granduncle of whom he'd never heard, a manor in the gray northlands of upper Scotland. Although some way's travel from Edinburgh, the manor became such a source of curiosity to its new owner that he took an immediate holiday from his business, a solicitor's firm, and presented himself on the doorstep of the old place. Only a caretaker remained of what must have been a sizable household staff, and this man would not be around much longer, if Josiah Ward had his say.

The man was tall and strongly built, but he had a lazy way of moving and, more important, a rather surly way of replying to questions posed by the new young master on his initial tour of the house. Several of the questions were such, of course, that the man might not be expected to know the answers—such as the identities of the people in some of the old portraits, exactly how many rooms were in the manor, the cost of maintenance—but the new owner became increasingly impatient as question after question was met with the reply that the caretaker had no idea. But it was not until they came to the end of the second-floor corridor and the door which was held fast by three strong but rusted bolts that Josiah Ward's temper really flared.

"That room, sir?" the caretaker asked. "It's a closet of some sort, I think. Empty, it is—bolted and empty. Always has been, I think. A room to be avoided."

As to why the room was to be avoided, the caretaker merely repeated that such was the case. No, he didn't know why, he just knew that those bolts had been in place for a long time before he came to the manor, and from what the other staff had said at the time he figured it was for a good reason. "But it is empty, sir. They say it always has been," he repeated. He then moved on, an exasperated Josiah Ward following along for the remainder of his tour of the manor.

It took little more than an hour for his curiosity to bring him back to that door, the proper tools with him to deal with the three bolts. There had to be something on the other side of that door, something worth hiding. A treasure perhaps? Josiah Ward didn't think so. No, it more than likely would be the evidence of some dark family secret. Perhaps it had been within the room that an insane member of the family had been kept, perhaps chained to the wall, his or her hysterical screams cutting through the dark night. Or perhaps the room had been used, long ago, for some dark rituals, the symbols of a trafficking in the Black Arts still upon the walls and floors. But *perhaps* wasn't good enough, of course. One simply had to know. . . .

First he tried to hammer the bolts back from their positions, not even bothering about the fact that such noise might bring the caretaker to the scene. The noise didn't, but neither did the hammer have much of an effect on the bolts. They were rusted too fast. The bolts would have to be pried from the wood. The task only took twenty minutes, but when it was done, Josiah Ward's clothing was soaked from the effort. As he opened the door, his heart was beating frantically with excitement. Then he scowled. The caretaker had been right. The room was small, it seemed to be nothing more than a closet, as the man had said. And it was empty. Completely empty, empty even of dust.

But why would an empty room be locked? There must be some explanation, Josiah Ward decided. And making that decision, he stepped into the room to investigate. After he did so . . .

The room was empty. Within the confines of its

clean white walls there was nothing . . . and no one. Completely empty except for one instant there when there was a sound . . . something which might have been the initial stage of a young man's shriek of terror. . . .

No, there is no trapdoor or any other mechanical trick device which "explains" this tale. As a matter of fact there's a house not far from your own in which there is a similar room, I'm told. You could, I suppose, investigate the matter yourself . . . if you're curious. . . .

IN THE GRAVEYARD ONE NIGHT

The story of Murphy and O'Toole

There are things that happen to people that are so disturbing that the story never gets told. What happened to Murphy and O'Toole, for example, happened many years before Murphy told the tale to his eldest son. By that time O'Toole had been dead for ten years, buried in the graveyard just outside their little village in County Cork. The same graveyard, but an older section, figures prominently in Murphy's tale. . . .

Both were young lads then, husky and strong, and both had young wives awaiting at home while, on the night of this story, Murphy and O'Toole were drinking with enthusiasm at The Green Inn. The inn and the grog were warm, but the night was quite the opposite. It was a horrible night, the whistling wind whipping ice-chilled rain in all directions so that it stabbed through even the thickest of clothing. Nonetheless, the time came when Murphy and O'Toole decided they had better leave the indoor warmth and get themselves home like the respectable husbands they were. But, just a door or two down from the inn, they stopped their homeward progress as, their faces huddled inside their jackets and caps, they almost collided with a large coal-black steed hitched to an open wagon.

The horse and wagon were not in motion. There appeared to be something lying down in the rear of the wagon, but no driver was nearby. At least, that is what they thought until a tall man in a black cloak appeared at their side. He, like Murphy and O'Toole, had his face hidden from the weather, but somehow the state of his clothing suggested that he'd been out in the rain for a far longer time than they. He looked to be drenched to the bone as he spoke to them.

The howling of the wind was so loud that the man had to shout, and Murphy and O'Toole on their part had to shout as well. He needed help. He had to move something. If they would help him, their reward would be considerable. The two young men tried to inquire as to just what had to be moved, but all they received in response was a pointed finger toward the wagon. The gesture was obvious. What had to be moved was there. Murphy and O'Toole climbed up into the wagon with the black-cloaked man. It was as the two men reached down to grapple with the large block of stone that their employer shook his head. No, not here, his gesture conveyed, with which he took a seat up front and lashed the fine black horse whose reactive lurch forward caused Murphy and O'-Toole to grasp the sides of the wagon in earnest. As they did so, they noticed that there was something else in the bottom of the wagon, something other than the stone. Two long-handled shovels. And now they recognized the stone for what it was. A grave marker.

The speed of the wagon through the barely visible

streets made Murphy and O'Toole uncomfortable, but they were even more uncomfortable when they recognized that they were passing between the two stone pillars which demarcated the entrance to the village cemetery. Murphy was on the verge of demanding an explanation from the driver when suddenly their movement halted and the tall, drenched man stepped down to the ground. Both young men made a move to follow, but a hand gesture stopped them. "The stone," the dark man said. "Here." Murphy and O'Toole looked at each other. They had come this far, after all. Why not? There was the matter of payment, too.

The stone was heavy, so much so that Murphy cursed under his breath that at the very least the man who had employed them could assist a little. But he didn't, unless you could count his bringing the two shovels from the wagon. Again his directions were short and to the point. The stone from the wagon was to be placed in the spot he indicated, right next to a stone which was of similar size and shape. He handed the shovels to the two young men. Both Murphy and O'Toole cursed this time, but they set into the work. When it was accomplished, the man inclined his head, as if bowing to the two of them. "And the payment?" O'Toole demanded. For an answer, the cloaked man merely pointed toward the wagon. Both Murphy and O'Toole looked in that direction. When, puzzled, they looked back, the cloaked man no longer was with them.

It didn't take them long to understand. The horse and wagon were to be their payment, one which was more than ample, considering the price fetched when they were sold. As for the disappearing man, they understood that also. The message was plain, right there on the headstone, you see. The family name matched that on the similar stone next to it, the stone of a woman who had died some five years previously. Under her name and the date was the inscription, *She was with her husband always*. The year of death on the man's stone was the current year, under which were these words: *Lost at sea, but never lost to her*. It was no wonder that the man had looked so . . . so wet. . . .

There is this moral to be drawn from the tale: If the dead ask for your help, they're willing to pay for it. At least, they are sometimes. . . .

THE BEAT OF LEATHER WINGS

The story of Petre

Fright is essentially an adult emotion. To be sure, children can be frightened, but the older one gets the more sources of terror become known to him. It is part of the process we call education, and, looking at the innocence of the very young, we are inclined to think it a better way of dealing with the world. But is it? The story of five-year-old Petre may help to clarify the matter. . . .

In the little village at the base of the Carpathian Mountains, the people were what you and I would call very superstitious, but, especially upon one night of the year, one could hardly miss witnessing the work of superstition and the symbolic prevention of terrible evils. The night was All Hallows' Eve.

Little Petre lived with his aunt and uncle, and, since there were no other children in the house, he was called upon to assist in the work which had to be completed before nightfall. The work consisted of fastening to the exterior and interior of the house—at each window and door—metal crosses and strings of garlic. All over the village, Petre's uncle told him, similar work was going on.

"It is the night of their coming," the uncle said. "They cannot enter where the cross and garlic command." The uncle would have explained more, but Petre's aunt intervened. There was no need to frighten the boy, she insisted. As long as the house was duly protected, all would be safe within. Besides, it had been many years since *they* had been seen or heard. Perhaps, because the village had been so protected for year after year, they now passed it by completely. So she said, but Petre did not miss the fact that both his aunt and uncle made a quick sign of the cross before their breasts even as she finished speaking.

The boy was sent to bed earlier than usual, the supper meal having been consumed in great haste. Before tucking him in, his aunt made certain that the window in Petre's room was locked, that the curtains were drawn, and that the garlic and the cross were positioned correctly. As the boy closed his eyes, visions of *them* danced in his mind.

He knew, of course, what caused the fear in the village. The vampires. An older boy had told him all about them. They lived in castles high in the mountains. They lived on the blood of others. The older boy even had an old book which had a drawing of a vampire. It was a horrible-looking thing with long teeth, a head almost like that of a goat but uglier, a tail like the Devil's and large leather wings shaped like the wings of a bat. No one in the village ever had seen a vampire personally, but obviously it was a terrible, terrible thing, Petre told himself as he buried his head deeper under the pillow.

It was totally dark and quiet in the house when Petre suddenly awoke. No one or nothing was stirring, but outside——it seemed, outside his very window——he could hear something. It sounded much like he thought heavy beating wings would sound . . . leather wings. Those ugly things, the vampires, were out there!

And then he remembered that no one in the village ever had seen a vampire. If that was so, how did anyone really know what they looked like? How could anyone draw a picture of a vampire such as the one in that book? The pictures couldn't be real, if nobody ever saw the thing it was supposed to be! But if they were out there now, then maybe he——Petre——could see them. And maybe they weren't as bad as his uncle and his aunt and the others all thought. He climbed down from his bed and moved to the window. When he opened the curtains, he saw them.

There were six of them, all standing upon the roof across the way. Petre could see them clearly in the moonlight. What's more, they could see him——they were looking at him right now. But the drawing was all wrong. They looked just like ordinary men and women. The men were dressed in dark rich-man's clothing, the women in long white flowing gowns. Their faces were smiling at him, and there were no long teeth or anything at all unusual——except perhaps for their eyes. Their red, burning eyes that seemed to be saying something to Petre. . . .

"Yes," Petre said suddenly. "You won't hurt anybody, I know that now." And, still quietly, because somehow he knew it was important not to wake up his uncle and aunt, he took down the cross and the garlic and then opened the window. Then he left the room. There were the other protections to remove. He had just completed clearing the entrance to the

bedroom of his uncle and aunt when he saw them—
the six—coming from his room. He wondered briefly
how they got from the roof they had been on to his
window. Then he knew. There were large batlike
wings attached to the six. And now they didn't look
at all like they had before. Their faces were changing,
but all the time their bright red eyes burned into his.

"It isn't fair!" Petre cried out. "You lied to me! I'll
tell my uncle!" But, of course, he didn't have to tell
his uncle. Petre's uncle and his aunt soon knew . . .
everything. . . .

Listen! Is that your child up in his room talking to
himself? Or, perhaps, is there someone—or something—up there with him? Shall we go and see. . . .

THE LAUGHING BUDDHA

The story of Vance Stillman

Do you ever wonder, when you pass through museum
rooms full of ancient artifacts, just how the museum
acquired some of the things they display? Assuredly,
most of the old items were acquired in aboveboard
transactions, but if the history of some of them were
known . . . Well, suffice it to say that there are men
such as Vance Stillman who earn rather substantial
incomes from plundering temples of the faithful.
Sometimes their work takes them to remote corners
of the world and sometimes, as was the case with
Vance Stillman, they not only find what they seek,
but something else. Stark terror. . . .

In the snow-covered heights of the Nepalese
Himalayas, Vance Stillman looked at the three-foot-
high statue of the altar within the modest but well-
kept temple. He first had heard of the "laughing Buddha" more than a month ago in Katmandu. A Bud-

dha of solid gold, it was said, a Buddha worshiped by a sect which was both small and strange in their doctrines. As he looked upon the statue, Vance Stillman made three deductions. One, it was not solid gold; one could see where the gold leaf had worn away from the baser metal of which the figure had been cast. Two, it was not really the Lord Buddha who was dipicted; the fierce eyes were narrowed in hatred and cruelty as was the laughing face which was as far from a Buddha's smile of solemnity as could be imagined. Three, whatever the seated figure might represent, it was very old—and therefore very valuable. Vance Stillman decided he would take the statue to civilization.

He anticpated little difficulty in enforcing his decision. The temple was guarded only by two thin priests who looked as if they were as old as the statue. Their cries of alarm as he stepped up to the altar and took the figure from its place above it were quickly quieted by the showing of the pistol he revealed from within his heavy coat. Even so, as Vance Stillman placed the figure into his backpack, one of the old priests attempted to block his exit from the temple. "No!" the old one said. "His place is in the mountains. He cannot be taken from them. *He will not go!*" Vance Stillman laughed as the barrel of his pistol cracked heavily into the old man's skull. The laughing Buddha, or whoever he was, was leaving—and he was leaving immediately.

It was not until the temple thief had been on his downward trail for ten minutes that he wondered whether or not the blow on the head had killed the old priest. Even then, he did not concern himself with the problem, he simply wondered. Of much more concern was the downfall of snow which was his companion at this stage of his descent. It would tend to slow him down, and a man could freeze in such weather if he slackened his pace. Vance Stillman laughed at his own concern. He had, after all, worked his trade in malaria-infested jungles. He had passed through nests of scorpions and rivers of crocodiles to earn his living. No, there was no reason to fear the pure, white snow. None at all. . . .

And then it happened. Stillman was moving along a narrow ledge, carefully placing foot before foot, when he felt it. A movement behind him, a sudden rustle and pressure upon his back—not loud, not heavy, but enough to make him turn. His eyes were difficult to believe. Somehow, someway, the flap on his backpack had come loose, although he was certain he had fastened it securely. But that wasn't the real concern. The statue . . . somehow, probably the wind, he thought . . . it was *out of the pack!* It seemed to pause for a moment in midair—and then it began to fall.

Vance Stillman's first cry was as he reached down to catch his treasure which he was certain was about to be lost to him forever down the cliffside. His second cry came as his reaching caused his balance to shift and his feet slipped out from under him—and he felt himself going over the side. A man of some agility, he flailed his limbs to thrust his body close to the slippery ice- and snow-covered rocks of the cliffside. He exhaled with relief when the sliding motion stopped, his boot soles finding a ledge which held. The smile which began to form on his face stopped in midmotion as he realized that the ledge he stood on was just that. A small outcropping which, while fortuitously placed to stop his plummeting to a certain death, neither went on to the left or to the right. There was nothing below, either—nothing but the sheer glistening ice wall to oblivion. The only possible route to safety was the way he had come. Upward. And as his eyes looked that way, Vance

Stillman cried out for a third time.

There above him—on the very edge of the ledge he had walked upon, the ledge which, being some twelve feet above him, he knew now he had no chance of reaching—there sat the golden figure. Stillman could see it clearly now, the snow having suddenly stopped. The statue's face looked straight down at him, its eyes narrowed in hate, its face contorted in disdain, its mouth curled into that hideous contortion of derision. It was, perhaps, Stillman's imagination, but as the treacherous ice-air of the mountains began to permeate his clothing and his skin, his glazed eyes seemed to see the figure move. And then his ears began playing tricks—or else they did in fact hear the laughter. But he had no chance to think about it, really, since that occurred moments before Vance Stillman froze to death. . . .

A fitting end, you say? I would think twice before voicing that opinion. I see, for example, that odd curio over on your table. True, you bought it from the native shopkeeper, all aboveboard, I'm sure. But have you considered . . . where *he* obtained the item.
. . .

DEATH CAN'T WAIT

The story of Henry Turner

There are times, usually in the early hours of the dark morning, when we are uncertain as to whether what we have experienced is real or is in fact but a dream. There are some who say that the quality of such an experience really is not important, asking us to consider the nature of dreams. Are not dreams real in themselves? How you and I might answer that question is not of much significance here. The point is that Henry Turner had his opinion and, given the nature of his dream—if that is what it was—who can blame him?

It was sometime after three that Wednesday morning when a sound in the room caused him to sit up in his bed. There, in the darkness, in a chair across the room, sat a figure whose face was very white. It was a man's face and it seemed to glow with a pale luminescence as the lips moved and spoke to Henry

101

Turner. "It is time, Henry. Three days from now, your time to join me will come."

Henry Turner had no doubt at all as to the identity of the owner of the pale face. He was staring into the hollow eyes of Death or an agent of the Grim Reaper. Even so, he was moved to protest. First, he was not all that old and he was not yet ready to die. Second, he simply could not die now—who would take care of his two maiden aunts who even now slept soundly in their room across the hall? But the pale white face showed no relenting. "Your responsibilities to your aunts are the reason you have received advance warning. You have three days in which to properly arrange your affairs—and theirs."

"But they can't get along without me!" Henry Turner shouted. And then he found that there was no one else in the room, none except himself. Cold sweat covered his body. A dream, that's what it had to be. He told himself that again and again as, restlessly, he tried to return to sleep. On the following days he convinced himself that it had been no more than a foolish dream, even though the memory of that pale white face remained in a dark corner of his mind, staying there, haunting him. Nonetheless, the weekend was coming up and he had promised his aunts that they would have their regular Saturday outing. They found it so refreshing to get away from the city for a day, enjoying the drive into the country, enjoying even the rush of expressway traffic. So it was that on Saturday, three days after Henry Turner dreamed of Death, his car was speeding northward, his mind focused on directing his vehicle and not overly attentive to the conversation of his aunts in the rear of the car—not until one of them called his attention to the strange hitchhiker up ahead on the right side of the road.

Like many hitchhikers he carried a sign, but it was

a curious sign. It did not specify a destination, but instead held a message: YOU WIN, AND LOSE. Instantly after absorbing the words, Henry's mind absorbed the man carrying the sign. A lean man dressed in black, with a pale white face—and hollow-looking eyes! Henry screamed, for he now knew what the words meant. Words to which his eyes now returned . . . a very bad thing to do in high-speed traffic when there was a sharp turn just coming up. . . .

Death came instantaneously in twisted metal and shattered glass. There were but three victims of the one-car accident. Henry Turner and the two aunts . . . who could not have gotten along without him. So, you see, Death can be thoughtful at times . . . even though it always insists on punctuality. . . .

HANGING HOUSE

The story of Cyril Sutton

There are those who scoff at stories of haunted houses. Cyril Sutton was among them and, although it cannot be said for certain whether the house in which he spent his last night was haunted, it can be said that it had its curious effects. It also can be said that Cyril Sutton scoffs no longer. . . .

Located just to the west of Richmond, Virginia, the house itself was of uncertain age, although it was said to have been built sometime in the very early nineteenth century. There had been several owners, each of whom had made plans to restore the place to its original condition, but none of the plans came to fruition. No one, you see, ever had remained alive in the house through a single night. There were tales of a curse, but they conflicted in almost every particular except one. The beginning of the series of deaths within the old walls was when someone's body was found hanging in the parlor.

The house, its furnishings representing several deliveries made by several new owners, was of strong and durable construction. At the time of our story it had been uninhabited for nine years, but all that was to change. So vowed Cyril Sutton, who had made a name for himself as a minor debunker of the supernatural, and who thought the stories of Hanging House were just so much balderdash.

That's how the house was known. Hanging House. Oh, some people referred to it as Death House or Blood House, but Hanging House was the most popular name, since that was how those who dared to spend a night within it were found the next morning. Hanging. And that was the primary reason for Cyril Sutton's skepticism. It was obvious to him, he pointed out, that the stories of the house formed quite a convenient outlet—not for anything supernatural, but for something quite natural. Murder.

At his press conference that last afternoon he explained what he meant. "People have enemies, all of us do. Therefore, some enemy who knows the tale about the house takes advantage of it. The first night the unsuspecting victim spends there, he is murdered—hanged, of course, to fulfill the requirements of the curse or whatever is supposed to be the cause." Asked if his theory did not presuppose an abundance of murderers, each with most accurate timing as well as similar methods of reasoning, Cyril Sutton asked in return whether anyone thought the act of hanging oneself was an easy way to die. "It takes a bit of managing, I daresay," he said. To an additional question—did he himself have any enemies who might employ the method posed by his theory?—he replied that he suspected he did. However, he had taken measures—in the form of a security patrol ringing the house—to assure that he would not be dispatched in an untimely manner by any human source intent on malice. In addition, he himself was going to carry an automatic pistol.

So it was that, armed with his pistol, a strong four-cell flashlight, and a small battery-operated tape recorder, Cyril Sutton entered Hanging House at nine fifteen. He entered quite alive, and the evidence has it that he remained in that state until some time after two in the morning. It was about two when the security guards heard the shots, you see. They converged on Hanging House at a run, but none of them entered the house itself. That was not in their bargain. Besides, they did not have to enter to see what had happened. But it wasn't until morning, when the security chief did deign to enter the house, that the additional evidence was discovered. The tape recorder. It said most of it, all in the voice of Cyril Sutton . . . almost as if he were speaking to his listeners from the other side of the Veil.

At nine thirty, he recorded the time and the following: "Well, here we are in Hanging House. Dismal sort of place." A laugh, quite cheerful. "I must say, having had a look around the rooms, that the previous owners deserved what they got. The place is a designer's nightmare, the overall theme being Early American Trash, ha-ha. I'm opening one of the windows now and you'll never guess the color of the curtains. It's an original color that I don't recall ever having seen before, I guess you'd have to call it Putrid Puce, ha-ha. . . ."

At ten, Cyril Sutton reported again, this time mentioning his boredom. At half-hour intervals over the next two hours, he did the same. At midnight, however, he spoke at length of the Witching Hour, closing with the note that "if anything happens, it should happen soon." At twelve thirty and one he

107

suggested that it was obvious that no witches were responsible for the supposed evils of the house. "They don't like to miss the midnight hour in doing their deeds," he laughed. But at one thirty he sounded bored again. "I should have had the foresight to bring a good book," he said. Then came the two o'clock recording.

It is a certainty that Cyril Sutton turned on the machine after he'd emptied his pistol, almost as an afterthought. It is also a certainty that he carried it with him until . . . until his fingers no longer could hold onto the device. In the increasingly hysterical words of Cyril Sutton, then:

". . . don't understand it. Almost like the wind, the sound . . . but that's not the worst. I tried shooting at them, but they still are there . . . figures of men . . . women, too, I think. It's hard to tell, they wear dark robes which cover everything but their hands. . . . Lord. what hands . . . white, thin, twisted. . . . And in those hands, held high up in the spaces above their heads . . . ropes . . . ropes in the form of nooses. . . .

"But the nooses aren't real! I've shot right through them as well as the carriers. And if they aren't real, they can't hurt me . . . *can't*! But—"

And then there is a scream on the tape and the sound of running feet—obviously those of Cyril Sutton. And then—a gagging, choking sound . . . a frantic beginning of a cry . . . and then the clatter of the machine striking the floor where it was found the next morning. Right there by the windows with the oddly colored drapes Cyril Sutton had commented upon, the windows which Cyril Sutton had intended to use as an exit from the house . . . the drapes among whose cords Cyril Sutton had become tangled . . . cords from which the body of Cyril Sutton now dangled by the throat. . . .

Ah, but ghost hunting can be a rewarding profession! If you're *personally* interested, I have a list of houses I might be persuaded to share with you. There are thirteen houses on the list. Seven of them are not really haunted. The problem, of course, is *which* seven. . . .

A SMALL TRICK

The story of Palmer the Great

I always enjoy stage magicians and their tricks. They provide not only entertainment but also mental stimulation. Attempting to unravel the explanations of how their effects are achieved is not always an easy task—unless the magician is of the order of Palmer the Great whose act offered little in the way of anything new or startling. Not until that one trick he performed which was most startling . . . expecially to himself. . . .

'He worked in nightclubs, Palmer the Great did, the nature of his places of work quite in harmony with the nature of his act—third class. He was working in Detroit when he read of Rosetti's visit to the city. Rosetti, the grand old master of magic. Rosetti, whose illusions were so spectacular that they puzzled even those magicians whose names were among the real greats of the industry. Rosetti, who long had quit the stage but who was known now and then to

111

help a younger member of his craft. And, although not young, Palmer the Great was in definite need of help, he decided.

Still, Palmer was surprised when the old man did not hesitate to invite him to his hotel suite. Arriving there a little after seven in the evening, Palmer explained his problem. He needed something new, a new trick which would catapult him from the bottom rungs of the profession they both shared. Rosetti laughed quietly, not unkindly, but in a way which told Palmer the Great that the old man understood. "You really wish to excel in the art?" he asked Palmer. "Would you, for example, wish to be able to perform a feat such as this?"

At the question, the old man solemnly uttered the well-worn magic word—Abracadabra—and thin appeared to snatch a golden coin from the air with his right hand. Palmer the Great looked puzzled. That was certainly nothing new. Even Palmer the Great could do it. But there was more to the trick, he now saw. In fact, he hardly could believe his own eyes as he watched—watched the old man . . . becoming smaller. Rosetti actually was shrinking in size! He had been about the same height as Palmer and now he was a head shorter, now two heads shorter. Then, with a sharp laugh, Rosetti repeated the magic word, this time producing his golden coin in his left hand. He began to grow taller.

When Rosetti was restored to normal size, Palmer the Great pleaded with the old man. "You must show me that trick! Such an effect would make me famous overnight!" The old man smiled. No, he said. Perfection in magic, as with anything else, took hard work and dedication. Palmer the Great was where he was in the field because he lacked these two essentials. No, he repeated. He neither would explain the effect to Palmer nor would he simply give him any other.

112

It was in a state of frustrated rage that Palmer the Great's fist crashed into the face of the older man. Rage, however, was replaced by fear when Rosetti did not get up from the floor, and it became apparent that he never would rise from it under his own power. The old man was dead. But by his head was the golden coin! Palmer the Great took it and ran from the hotel room.

It was not until he was in the middle of his nightclub act that night that he decided to give the golden coin a try. He had, after all, nothing to lose. At worst, it would be just an appearing-coin trick. But, if somehow, he could make Rosetti's trick work. . . . if, as the thought just then struck him, it wasn't just a trick, but the coin itself were . . . magic . . . He laughed at the idea, then shook his head. Suppose it *were* magic, the coin itself? Then he—anyone—could do it. "Abracadabra!" Palmer the Great shouted—and he produced the coin by seeming to pluck it from the air. He felt the change at the exact moment someone in his audience gasped. There were more cries of surprise now as, yes, the room seemed to get larger around him. It worked! It *was* magic, real magic! Palmer the Great was on his way to becoming *really* great! But this first time it would be best not to overdo it, not to reduce himself too much. He slipped the coin from his right hand to his left. He again said the magic word, this time with the solemnity which befit a first-class magician. Then he said the word again—and again!

He had been screaming for more than five seconds, getting smaller by the instant, when it came to him— the old man must have had two coins, one to reduce his size and the other to . . . It was then that Palmer the Great screamed even more loudly, leading the chorus of cries which came from all those who gathered around him . . . all those gigantic people

113

who seemed to loom larger and larger. . . .

Have you ever thought of dabbling in sleight of hand? If you do, the tale of Palmer the Great is one to remember. Its moral of thoroughness is most clear. Half a trick decidedly is not better than none. . . .

DOWN TO THE SEA IN SCREAMS

The story of John and Deborah Grover

It is said that all life came from the sea, that down in the dark depths the original life forms still inhabit the mutating ooze. But if the sea is so bountiful, why is it the source of so much fear? Is it, perhaps, because where there is life there also is death? Or is it because the world under the waves is closed to most of us—and that now and then, when we get a glimpse of what lies at the sea bottom . . . or when from the depths something moves shoreward . . . its impact upon us is such that it would have been far better for the known to remain as it was . . . unknown?

John and Deborah Grover might be in a position to enlighten us . . . or I should say that they might *have been*. . . .

It was a tiny New England coastal village, one which appealed to the Grovers because it looked so small and lonely there on the map. A far cry from

Boston, which was what they were looking for. Young newlyweds are like that. They seek to be alone, which, in the Grovers' case, would have been fine—if they had not also wished additional adventures.

The man who sold fishing bait and tackle was stern in his warning. "For this one week we do no crabbing, nor any other type of fishing. We honor the elder god by this, and none venture into the sea to ensnare his little brothers." To John and Deborah the advice was nonsense. They had this one week before returning to Boston and their city jobs. No, they would not be dissuaded by superstitious claptrap, even though the local resident, repeating his warning, refused to rent them a boat.

By the late afternoon of their first day, they had done well. Although confined to the shoreline, they had a sizable catch of crabs, and they were about ready to quit when they noticed the boat. A small rowboat which seemed to be drifting aimlessly along the shoreline—a boat which was empty. No, not quite, they found. For as they waded out a bit to intercept the vessel, they discovered that, although there was no one guiding the boat, there were things aboard. Namely the oars, a tackle box and two sturdy fishing poles. Without a word, John and Deborah agreed that this afforded them an excellent opportunity to try their luck a ways out from the shore. Besides, they couldn't let the boat just drift on, could they? They climbed aboard, John using the oars to guide the vessel. Deborah, meanwhile, affixed an artificial lure to her line and cast out to the rear of the boat. Immediately she squealed with joy, then she scowled.

Whatever she had hooked into was of some size, judging by the way her pole bent. But when she tried to reel in her line, the spool didn't move. It seemed to be jammed. Releasing the oars, John moved to assist his wife. It was just as he was about to take the pole from her that there was a snapping sound and they both cried out in pain. Their four hands were on the pole and through their palms—completely through—were strong steel hooks, very effectively barbed, which had snapped upward from the handle portion on the rod. It was then that whatever was on the other end of the line jerked hard and the boat capsized, spilling Deborah and John over the side and into the waves. Screaming and choking, their terror-filled minds wondered what was coming next.

They didn't wonder long. For, hooks baited and taken, the fisherman who had them now was slowly beginning to reel in the catch. . . .

Do you enjoy fishing? If so, I suggest that when you're out in your boat and you see something dark—something large and shapeless—under the surface that you reel in your line rather quickly. There are some things . . . even in the smallest of lakes and rivers . . . that it would be best not to hook into. . . .

THE PHANTOM FIDDLER

The story of Theodore and Thayer

There is something mysterious about twins, especially identical twins. Oh, there are scientific explanations as to why some twins are so in tune with each other. But rational explanations evaporate when twins look at each other in that special way, a way which you know means that they are communicating with each other . . . in eerie silence. And shall we try to explain, in logical terms, what really happened when twelve-year-old Thayer played the violin?

The violin was not Thayer's. No, the instrument was the treasured possession of his twin brother, Theodore. And the excitement in their home was in high pitch, as it was almost time for that looked-for night at the city music hall when Theodore was to appear as a soloist. For the boy, even at twelve, played the violin like a master, and the conductor of the city orchestra had publicly said that he'd heard no one

better in all his years in music. But the euphoria of
the family was short-lived. The day prior to the long-
awaited concert, Theodore was struck down and
killed by an automobile. Amidst the grieving,
someone mentioned that, as a result of the tragedy,
the concert might have to be canceled.

It was then that Thayer announced that he would
appear in his brother's stead, an announcement
which drew sad smiles from those who heard it. For
while Theodore had been inclined to music and other
artistic pursuits, his look-alike brother had been more
devoted to rough sports. Thayer played no musical
instrument at all. He had never once touched his
brother's violin, his parents would have sworn to it.
"Nonetheless," Thayer insisted, "I shall appear on
the music hall stage tomorrow night."

The conductor, of course, had very real reserva-
tions. But finally, due to his respect for the dead
youth, he agreed that the concert would be given and
that Thayer could sit among the orchestra members—and that, yes, he could hold his brother's
violin. But there was to be no playing by Thayer, that
was to be clearly understood. The particular piece
which was to feature Theodore was not to be performed. Thayer finally agreed to these terms, although there was something in his face which, if
anyone had looked closely, would have been slightly
disturbing. . . .

All went well during the first two-thirds of the program. Thayer did exactly as he was told. He sat
solemnly if a bit disinterestedly in the violin section
as number after number drew the expected amount of
polite applause from the audience. Then suddenly a
smile formed on the boy's face. The conductor had
turned to the audience and was explaining that, due
to young Theodore's tragic accident, the next selection noted on the printed program was to be deleted.

It was then that Thayer stood—and began to play.

Audience and orchestra were stunned. The conductor, his eyes wide with noncomprehension, nonetheless lifted his baton. The other instruments came in somewhat clumsily behind the violin, but within moments the selection was being performed as it was intended to be. The violin in Thayer's hands sang out gloriously, its full tones bringing tears of sorrow and tears of joy alternately to those who filled the music hall. When the last notes came triumphantly from the strings of the violin, the applause was thunderous. The standing ovation rocked the very walls of the building as Thayer's mother and father rushed out onto the stage. Shouts of *encore!* began in earnest, then the conductor gestured the audience to silence. He turned to Thayer, a questioning look on his face. The boy shook his head and handed the instrument to his mother.

"I'm sorry," he said. "Just the one time . . . that's all we could work it. . . ."

What is your logical explanation for what is a true story? I'd be most interested to hear it. While we speak, do you mind if we listen to a recording of music . . . played by a young violinist who never played ever again. . . .

THE DEAD REST UNEASILY TONIGHT

The story of Thomas Tilden

We hear so much today of minority rights and there is, I suppose, much merit in these discussions. But have we paid enough mind to the rights of the majority—by which I mean the *greatest* majority . . . the dead? Perhaps you think I am joking. If so, it is best that I tell you what happened to Thomas Tilden who also might have thought I was joking. In other days, he might have, but not today. No, there would be little chance of that. . . .

Thomas Tilden liked to call himself a developer. By Thomas Tilden's definition, a developer is one who obtains effective control over a piece of real estate and, doing something with it to increase its value (in some cases merely effective promotion), then selling said piece of real estate for a sizable profit. Thomas Tilden did very well at being a developer for three excellent reasons. One, he worked hard.

Two, he was quite shrewd in his dealings. Three, he had marshaled enough political pull to manipulate those elements of legal machinery which might otherwise be obstructive to Thomas Tilden's having his way. Thus he expected little difficulty when he decided that, in order to carry out a large and expensive housing project, an old but otherwise unassuming church would have to be relocated—complete with the bodies in the church cemetery. . . .

Oh, there was a bit of public clamor, to be sure. The people who formed the church congregation wrote angry letters of protest to the city officials and to the newspaper. They even picketed the city hall. But they were, after all, mostly old people, not very wealthy, and thus not very important to the city fathers. Not when contrasted with the likes of Thomas Tilden in any case. There was very little in the way of doubt how the matter was going to turn out. The congregation and their dead simply would have to be satisfied with the new site which had been picked out for them. All costs of relocation, including construction of the new church and reburial of the deceased, were to be borne by the Tilden interests, naturally. Thus as usual the needs of progress would be served. Or so Thomas Tilden thought. . . .

It was quite late when the developer was sitting in his private office, going over the fine print of the papers which, when signed the next day, would cement the movement of the church and graves. A sound in the outer office made Thomas Tilden look up from his paper work. There were more sounds . . . shuffling sounds . . . sounds of feet moving across the floor out there. Cautiously, Thomas Tilden rose from his chair. "Who's there?" he asked.

Slowly the door connecting the two rooms opened. The man who entered stood in the shadows, beyond the range of the goosenecked lamp on the desk. As

v
je